Love Found at Cranberry Cove

June Foster

ISBN: 978-1-952661-84-6

"Trust in the Lord with all your heart and lean not on your own understanding. In all your ways submit to Him, and He will make your paths straight." Proverbs 3:5-6 NIV

Chapter One

Blake Sloan wrinkled his nose. The odor of pine antiseptic and bleach reminded him of his whereabouts—the cardiac unit of Seattle General Hospital. The call from Dad earlier this morning still rang in his ears—Grandpa was hospitalized again. The second time in two years was too much. He gripped his fingers into tight balls. No, one heart attack in a lifetime was too much.

The corridors were quiet, and he heard only the click of his shoes as he veered to the left. At the end, he pulled in a deep breath. In what condition would he find Grandpa?

Propped up in bed, the older man lay against the pillows, eyes closed. Instead of his usual tan, a pasty white colored his skin, and tubes ran to his nostrils.

Blake whispered, his heart pounding with each syllable. "Grandpa, are you okay?" Was he conscience?

Jonas Sloan's eyes fluttered open and a slight smile emerged. "Blake, my boy." He held out his hand. "I'm glad you're here."

Blake stepped closer to the bed, gripped the

wrinkled hand, and swallowed the regret that threatened to wobble his voice. "How'd you wind up here again?" He faked a chuckle.

"Oh, you know doctors these days. I had a little chest pain, and my cardiologist told me to check into the hospital."

"Dad said you'd had a heart attack." A condition that could lead to death. Blake's stomach churned.

"Just a little pressure in my chest. Doc wanted me to stay a few days—as a precaution." Grandpa squeezed Blake's hand. "Don't worry, son. I'm fine. The good Lord isn't calling me home yet."

Movement sounded behind Blake, and he turned to see his father at the door. "Hello, Dad."

Dad patted Blake's shoulder and peered at Grandpa. "How are you feeling?"

"I'm fine. I'm fine." Grandpa brushed his hand through the air.

Dad checked his watch and then neared Grandpa's bed. "The rest will do you good."

Grandpa sat up higher against the pillow. "Gerald, I'd like to see you slow down, also. Your mind is always on those ships."

"You ran this company for years." Dad firmed his lips. "You ought to know the responsibilities."

"That's exactly why I say don't push yourself as hard as you do. Do you want to end up in a hospital like me?" Grandpa wrinkled his brow.

Blake's sentiments exactly, but he couldn't tell his father. For months, Blake had driven himself at a pace equivalent to Dad's. The fleet of ships and Dad's company occupied his mind twenty-four seven. Was that really what he wanted for his life?

Dad thrust his hands in his pockets and shifted his weight from one foot to the other. "Did I tell you we're adding a fourth vessel to our fleet? I have an appointment with the finance man in an hour."

Blake bristled. Had Dad forgot about encouraging Grandpa who lay in a hospital bed?

"On Saturday?" Grandpa glowered. "Have you signed the final papers? I'd strongly advise against the move. At least for now."

"There've been changes since you ran the company." Dad raised his voice. "We're expanding as well as increasing the number of clients we service. Face it, we can't slow down progress."

Blake gritted his teeth. He hated the times when Dad dismissed his Grandpa's opinions.

Grandpa pounded his palm with his fist. "Gerald, I know I'm not involved with operations now but... " He coughed and gripped his chest.

A nurse rushed into room and glared at Dad. "Excuse me, but Mr. Sloan needs to rest."

Dad ran his hand through his hair and muttered something that sounded like *sorry*. He headed out the door.

Blake held his palms up and hoped she recognized his pleading tone, how much it meant to him to say good-bye. "I only need a few more minutes with my grandfather."

She eyed him and stepped to the door. "All right. But please keep your voice down."

"Sure." Blake clasped his grandpa's shoulder. "I'm sorry about Dad. He frustrates me sometimes." Blake gazed into his grandfather's kind eyes. "I stayed behind to tell you I love you."

"I love you, too, Blake." Grandpa grasped Blake's arm. "Let this old man give you some guidance. You won't be happy unless you're doing what the Lord above has planned for you. Does your job fulfill you?"

"Why do you ask?" Did Grandpa sense what was in Blake's heart?

"Call it a hunch." He chuckled.

Blake's throat clogged. Grandpa knew him so well. "I'm beginning to realize when I went to work for Dad after college instead of doing a tour of duty in the military, I was following Dad's dream, not my own."

Grandpa patted his hand. "Seek God and see where He leads you."

Talk to God? I doubt that. "I promise I will." He leaned down and kissed Grandpa's wrinkled forehead.

"Look, Blake. I'm fine and will be out of the hospital in a day or two. I want you to pursue your dreams—those things God's put on your heart."

Out on the sidewalk in front of the hospital, Blake pulled out his cell phone and punched the number he needed, only to get his voice mail. "Dad, this is Blake. I'm taking some time off. I need to get away—time to think."

Blake drove to his apartment and packed a bag. He took I-5 south. The road would decide his destination.

Monday morning, Gracie Mayberry's bike tires crunched on the gravel when she rolled up to her usual parking place at The Inn at Cranberry Cove. She hopped off and set the kickstand, shivering from the steady mist that had fallen her entire ride. The entrance to the kitchen was around the corner. The aroma of rich coffee and cinnamon rolls tempted her appetite— exactly what she needed right now. She shook the droplets off her raincoat and marched in. "Hey, Mom. Got any leftovers?"

Mom's auburn curls bounced as she pressed the button on the dishwasher and smiled. "Hey, honey. Saved you some."

"I bet James and Ashton appreciate you. You've been a lifesaver—especially since Ashton's doctor ordered her to remain on bedrest."

"She could give birth any day now." Mom swiped the spotless counter one more time. "They're grateful for you, too. James said he wasn't sure what they would've done if you hadn't taken a leave of absence from Starbucks and come to help at the inn. Your willingness to clean rooms is a godsend."

"I want to help out." To merely set foot in the beautiful old inn thrilled her. Gracie stared out the gray shuttered window to the back deck that extended along the length the house. The B and B was Ashton's dream, and though Gracie enjoyed her work, her goal still loomed in the future—to attend Oceanview Community and study marine biology. After Mom and Dad no longer needed her help and as soon as she saved up enough money, she could pursue her degree.

Mom gave Gracie a hug. "Are you okay?"

"Of course. I was just thinking about you and Dad. I'm blessed to have you as my family." Gracie followed Mom into the dining room.

Mom opened the china cabinet and set out the hand-painted salad bowls and dinner plates in preparation for the evening meal. "Honey, I know you want to enroll in college. You will one day soon—as soon as Dad..." Mom shook her head and clamped her mouth shut.

Gracie gave Mom a weak smile and picked up the pile of dinner plates. "It's understandable with him in his wheelchair and all." No need to remind her mother that Dad never tried to get out of the chair or go anywhere much less take a job.

Mom returned to the kitchen and set the bowls on the counter. "Your father was such a handsome man when I married him." She laughed. "You should've seen him in his army uniform. Good looking and strong. He used to carry me in his arms as if I didn't weigh an ounce. Then the Afghanistan War changed all that."

Gracie set the plates next to the bowls. "Don't dwell on the past. Dad's still with us, and that's all that matters."

"You're right." Mom brushed a tear from her cheek. "Speaking of work, Ashton asked us to pay close attention to her jade plants in the dining room. She wants us to fertilize them. I think there's some extra fertilizer spikes in the tool shed."

"I'll get right on it."

"After that, two of the upstairs guest rooms need cleaning." As if she'd never shed a tear only moments earlier, Mom smiled. "Ashton said she wouldn't know what to do without you."

Gracie grinned, hoping not to show her disappointment that her schooling would be delayed. She stepped out onto the deck and then gave herself a mental kick. If she were in Ashton's shoes, she'd want someone's help. The Savior said He came into the world to serve and not to be served. Couldn't she do the same?

She sniffed the scent of the early spring rain and pulled an umbrella from the vase stand, holding the waterproof nylon panels over her head against the moisture.

She shivered as she slogged on the grassy slope beyond the deck to the tool shed. She'd be glad when summer showed up. Anxious to get out of the cold sooner, she picked up her pace. Her heel slid and both feet slipped beneath her. With a plop, she fell into a rain puddle, backside first, jeans and shoes absorbing water like a paper towel.

"Oh, great." She tried to hold the umbrella with one hand and push up with the other. Thankfully, no one was near enough to witness her graceless plunge.

"Here, let me help you." A man reached toward her with his large, masculine hand.

Blake restrained the chuckle that threatened. He couldn't make fun of the lovely lady who'd just taken a dive onto the slippery grass. "Are you okay?"

Red stained her cheeks as she accepted his hand. "I, er, yeah, I'm fine." She stomped her feet and brushed off her jacket.

"You had quite a tumble." He tried to disguise his amusement.

"I slipped on the grass." She swatted at her jeans, no doubt trying to brush off the accumulated mud.

Blake reached for the umbrella and held the protection over her. "Where were you headed?"

"To the tool shed. I came to get some fertilizer spikes from the storeroom, but that can wait. I better change clothes." At the deck, she climbed the stairs.

"Are you sure you're okay?"

"Nothing broken." She stuck out her hand. "I'm Gracie Mayberry. You must be a guest. I hope you have a nice stay."

"Thanks. I'm Blake Sloan."

Chapter Two

Gracie slipped off her raincoat by the back door of the small cottage where she lived with Mom and Dad. The place was home, and she didn't need opulence. She had two loving parents.

In the mud room, she kicked off her shoes. What a klutz. Landing in a puddle of rainwater, bottom side down, in front of that handsome guest. Though she didn't see him laughing over her plight, he likely did after she walked inside the inn.

"Dad, I'm home." She tramped into the living room glad water didn't drip from her jeans onto the hardwood floor. "I need to take a shower and change clothes. I had a little accident at the inn." Flames blazing in the brick fireplace heated the room as well as her cheeks.

"Over here, Gracie." Dad's chair was parked in front of the window that looked out onto the forest surrounding much of Cranberry Cove. He wheeled around, the home phone set in his lap. "What happened to you?" He snickered.

"Don't ask." She rolled her eyes. "I fell in the mud."

"Gracie Lynn Mayberry. Aren't you a little old for

playing in the dirt?"

"Cute, Dad." She glanced again at the phone in his lap. "Making phone calls?"

"No." He rolled to the table and replaced the phone speaker on the charger. "Did you try to call today?"

"No, not today." She quirked her brow.

He glanced toward the phone set. "This thing has been ringing all morning. The screen says unknown. When I pick up, I hear breathing and then a click."

Gracie walked toward the cabinet and lifted the receiver. "Hmm." She replaced the phone. "If this keeps up, I vote that we disconnect our landline."

Dad nodded. "I suppose you're right, but I can't imagine who's calling."

Gracie shrugged. "Probably some prankster who doesn't have anything better to do."

Blake pulled in a long breath of salt air scented with the fresh aroma of evergreens and pines. For an entire hour during his walk around the inn's grounds, he didn't think of Sloan and Sloan once. He'd made a good decision to head south, toward the coast.

Answers he sought eluded him like chasing butterflies. If he knew God better, this would be the time to talk to Him. But how was he supposed to speak about the direction his life should go—with a stranger? He was next in line to run his father's powerful company, but was that what he wanted? Grandpa encouraged him to follow what God called him to do. Blake gazed upward. "God, help me to know you better. Give me direction." He only heard silence then he shrugged.

Inside the inn's foyer, he ambled toward the bottom step of the magnificent stairway which led to the second floor. Halfway up at the landing, he paused to gaze at the intricate stained-glass window. He'd only seen such beautiful work in a cathedral once when he went to Italy with Mom and Dad on vacation. Blue and green squares with a yellow rose within each formed the perimeter. Two intertwined knots and a dove flying upward filled the middle part of the glass.

At the top of the stairs, he strolled down the hall. Someone moved about in the room before his. The attractive redhead who'd fallen into the rain puddle set a stack of towels on the bed and then headed into the hall.

"Hello, again, Gracie."

"Oh." She jumped, and her mouth dropped open, her lovely azure eyes flashing.

He rubbed the back of his neck. "I'm sorry to have startled you."

"No. Just surprised me. I'm still a little embarrassed about my clumsy spill onto the ground."

Blake studied her cheeks which had turned a soft shade of pink. "The cutest tumble I've seen in a long time." He held up his hands in surrender. "But I don't remember a thing about it anymore."

She grinned. "How's your stay going?"

"I like Cranberry Cove. I think I'll leave Seattle and move here." Why had he said that? The words were the first thing out of his mouth.

Gracie closed the door to the room next to his. "I hope you have a nice visit." Obviously in no mood to chat, she gathered some cleaning supplies and glanced toward the staircase at the end of the hall.

Behind her on the wall, Blake spotted a picture. "That's Iwo Jima."

She followed his gaze. "The famous painting of the soldiers and the flag always brings chills to my arms. The previous owner was an art lover, and she appreciated the military."

"I do, as well." His insides warmed, and he lifted his chin. "My grandfather was in the marines."

Her face brightened. "If you have time while you're here, you should visit the war museum down at the wharf. The exhibits are inspiring. If you like history, you'll enjoy it."

Blake cleared his throat and mustered his courage. "I hope you don't think I'm forward, but does your job description at the inn include tour guide?"

"I'm here temporarily while the owner has her baby, but I'd be happy to show you the wharf where all the sea-going boats are docked and the restaurants—if I'm not too busy playing in mud puddles." She chuckled. "There are other places you could visit as well. The lighthouse or MarineWorld in Oceanview if you don't mind driving. There are plenty of biking trails, too."

Her change in attitude fascinated him. Was it because he told her about his grandpa and the military? "You said you're working here temporarily. What occupies the rest of your time?"

"Oh," she glanced at her shoes, "I'm hoping to save enough money to go to Oceanview Community College. I'd like to get a degree in Marine Science." She stared at something over his shoulder. "Maybe train and perform with the sea animals."

"It's a unique profession not everyone could qualify

for." Something about this perky, petite woman fascinated him—but what? Determination, independence. "Can we set a time to go to the wharf tomorrow?"

"Sure. I'll check with my mother. She's the head housekeeper and cook. If I'm not scheduled for anything, I can."

Gracie returned to the kitchen and glanced around for Mom. The thought of showing Blake the wharf sounded more appealing by the moment. Though his request seemed a little bold, Blake appeared to be sincere. Wouldn't hurt to be kind to a guest.

"Mother, where are you?"

The whirling of the washing machine sounded from the laundry room off the kitchen. Gracie peeked in at her mother stuffing towels in the dryer.

"Am I doing anything tomorrow, probably in the afternoon? One of the guests asked me to show him the wharf." Like during childhood, she was tempted to beg—*say yes, say yes.*

Mom frowned, as if she didn't know Gracie.

"Are you okay?"

Mom's vacant gaze said she was a hundred miles away. "What?" Like waking up from a dream, she stared at Gracie. "What did you say, dear?"

"I asked if I could take a guest to the wharf tomorrow."

Her mother wiped her hands on her apron more times than necessary. "Uh huh."

Gracie didn't have a clue as to what bothered her. "Okay, I'm making plans with Blake Sloan tomorrow. Let me know if anything else comes up." Gracie started out of the kitchen.

"Gracie."

Gracie swiveled around.

Mom's eyes widened, and she raised her voice. "Be careful wherever you go. What if he... " Mom's chest fell. "Please. Stay safe."

Gracie stepped back in the room and hugged her mom. "Sure, Mom."

What in the world had gotten into her mother? She said *he*. Did she think Blake would harm her?

That night, Gracie fingered the lace curtains at the window in her small bedroom at the back of the house. She glanced up, peering at the stary sky. How had God created the universe? She couldn't wrap her mind around it.

Blake, the nice-looking guy staying at the inn, distracted her thoughts. He'd said he wanted to move to Cranberry Cove. Or was it idle talk? Why would a man from the big city of Seattle want to live in her small village? He obviously appreciated the military since he'd pointed out the picture of Iwo Jima and mentioned his grandpa had served in the marines.

She sighed as his eyes, the color of coffee with cream, flittered into her mind. His face had seemed to speak of longing—or doubt. She wouldn't mind knowing what went on in his head.

Movement at the edge of the forest caught her attention. A deer? Like a shadow, someone or something scurried from one tree to the next.

Gracie reached for her bedside lamp and switched off the light. She peered out the window again.

A cloud floated over the moon and then a beam cast a slender ray on the woods behind the house. A figure darted from a Douglas fir into the blackness of the forest.

Gracie shivered. Someone was out there, and she had no idea why.

Surely, Blake wouldn't spy on her. No. He didn't even know where she lived, but Mom had been nervous. That was it. Mom's behavior had made her see things. Gracie dismissed the thought and crawled into bed. After a few minutes, she crept to the window again. Only blackness clothed the sky. Trees from moments ago were no longer visible. Yes. Her imagination had deceived her. The shadows could play tricks sometimes.

Chapter Three

Blake held the door as Gracie swung her shapely legs around and stepped out of his car. A sign to his left indicated The Wharf of Cranberry Cove.

A puff of ocean breeze lifted a strand of her auburn hair. "I usually like to walk to the end of the boardwalk and back." She pointed toward a line of docked boats.

They took a short flight of stairs to the pier and set out on the wooden walkway. The second building on his right displayed a sign: Cranberry Cove Museum of War. "You mentioned the exhibit. One day before I go back to Seattle, I'd like to take the tour. Have you been there?"

"Yes, a few times. I want to go back."

He walked closer to the entrance and glanced at the operating hours. "I am in awe the men and women who fought to keep our country free and… well, I regret I wasn't one of them."

"You wanted to join a branch of the military?"

"Looking back now, I wish I had followed in my grandpa's footsteps."

"I've always believed God put deep desires in our

hearts." She fingered a cross around her neck.

He wasn't so sure God was responsible but perhaps his grandfather's example had been. "But even now there's got to be something I could do to make a difference."

"Like what?"

He glanced over her shoulder at a seagull circling through the air. The bird settled on a wooden stake protruding from the water. "I've thought about a non-profit to aid wounded vets. Perhaps a DAV office." He hadn't planned to tell her about the hopes he'd mulled over for months, but she seemed to want to know.

Gracie's face brightened, and her gaze spoke of pride. "It's a great idea. I think about our wounded heroes daily."

What had she meant? If she wanted to say more, she would.

The sunrays lit the water, giving the appearance of diamonds dancing on the ocean's surface. He couldn't ask for a better day. The beautiful young woman by his side gave him reason to forget about the problems at home.

Gracie adjusted her wide-brimmed straw hat which protected her fair skin as they neared the water. "Tell me about your family. What do you do when you're not visiting Cranberry Cove?"

She made polite conversation, he was sure, but he didn't want to mention his opulent lifestyle at home. She seemed to bring out a different side of him, the real him or at least the person he wanted to be. "I work for my father. We run a company that's been in our family since my great grandfather who was in the whaling business. We have on-board facilities for fish processing and freezing."

"Sure, I've heard of that type of vessel. They're called factory ships, right?"

"Yes." He'd talked enough about himself. "What about your family?"

Gracie seemed to focus on a fishing vessel toward the end of the pier as it slowly docked. "My mom divorced my biological father when I was one. She met and married Dad Mayberry two years later. He adopted me, and he's the only father I've ever known." She took a breath. "I don't remember what my first father looks like, and Mom never speaks of him or her life back then."

Her emphatic tone of voice warned him. He wouldn't ask anything more about her biological father since the subject sounded like a touchy one. "What kind of work does Mr. Mayberry do?"

A frown creased her brow for a moment then disappeared. "He's disabled. He lost both legs in Afghanistan five years ago." She folded her hands at her waist. "I think Dad suffers from PTSD, but he refuses to get a diagnosis."

Blake instinctively reached toward her and then withdrew his hand. "Now I know what you meant when you said you were reminded daily."

She nodded. "He gets a pension from the VA, but the funds aren't enough these days, especially in Washington state with the high cost of living. Mom and I have tried to encourage him to seek the VA for employment training assistance, but in my opinion, he's lost his confidence." She rubbed the side of her forehead. "I didn't mean to unload on you."

"Hey, no worries, Gracie." Finances wasn't

something that concerned Blake. Money was a part of life he took for granted. "So, your mom and you both work at the inn for now."

"Yes. She's usually happy, even humming a tune as she works. But yesterday, when I checked with her about going to the wharf, she was in a mood. Distracted, worried about something. I have no idea what. She even told me to be careful." She tapped her head. "There I go again."

"I guess I'm just a good listener." Blake laughed. "I hope she wasn't concerned about you hanging out with me. My parents raised me to respect women. My father has his faults, but he's a great role model in the way he treats Mom."

Gracie shook her head. "I'm sure that's not the problem. My mother will open up eventually. She never holds secrets from me."

The wooden wharf with a variety of boats ran along the shoreline. A large commercial trawler slowly pulled alongside another smaller vessel and docked. Several minutes later, a couple of guys dressed in oilskin jackets and chest waders tied the ship with heavy ropes.

"The majority of the boats that dock here at the wharf are fishing vessels." Gracie grasped the brim of her hat as a gust of ocean breeze whirled around them. "Some sell fresh fish to the local restaurants. There are a few sport fishermen who depart from Cranberry Cove as well."

A muscular guy with sandy hair stepped off the trawler and spoke to one of the deck hands.

Wait a minute. He looked familiar. Blake took a few steps toward the man then stopped. He pointed toward the newly arrived vessel. "I think I know the captain of that trawler. He's someone I went to high school with. Ryder Langston. He was a freshman, and I was a sophomore. Then he moved away—to Tacoma."

Gracie shaded her eyes. "Looks like your buddy is a commercial fisherman now."

An older man disembarked from the small, rusted aluminum boat next to the trawler.

Ryder neared him, and the two seemed to start up a conversation. Ryder rested his hand on the old fisherman's shoulder and bowed his head. After a few minutes, he gave the man an envelope.

Blake turned to Gracie. "I wonder what that was about."

Gracie smiled. "I'd say Ryder prayed for him."

"Interesting. Do you know the old guy?"

"No, I've never seen him before, but then I don't come to the wharf a lot." She frowned as she continued to peer at Ryder and the other man still in conversation.

Then the old fisherman in dusty jeans and a worn-out jacket shook Ryder's hand. He looked up from the envelope Ryder had given him and stared in their direction. He gaped and widened his eyes.

"Hmm. Something has the old fisherman concerned from the looks of his expression. Let's go talk to Ryder." He grasped Gracie's hand, and the old man rushed toward his boat, disappearing into the cabin.

"That was strange." Gracie bit her lip. "Almost like he knew one of us."

"Yeah." They neared his friend. "Hey, Ryder Langston. Is that you?"

Ryder turned around and squinted. "Blake? Blake Sloan." He stepped closer and held out his hand. "Haven't seen you since high school. How's it going?"

"I'm well."

"What are you up to these days?" Ryder grinned.

"I work for my dad now." No way he'd brag about his high paying job in Sloan Towers located in downtown Seattle. Blake shook his hand and smiled toward Gracie. "Do you know Gracie Mayberry?"

Ryder nodded toward Gracie. "No, but it's nice to meet you."

Gracie tucked a strand of hair behind her ear. "Do you have a card? I'd like to put you in touch with the owners of The Inn at Cranberry Cove. They might like to order some of your fresh fish."

"Of course. I always welcome new customers. But right now, I could sure use a fishing supply store on the wharf. I need to replace some netting, so I'll have to wait until I go up the coast to Oceanview."

Blake squinted with the sun as he glanced toward the large trawler bobbing up and down at the pier as an idea formed in his mind. "A fishing supply store would be helpful for the commercial fishermen in the area as well as boost the Cove's economy."

"I like the idea, Blake." Gracie patted his arm. "I'm sure the business would do well."

Like flame lighting a candle, the notion sparked. He could open a store and sell fishing supplies. Then he caught his breath. His heart told him he wanted to assist wounded vets. Would it be feasible to manage both? Was he capable of it? As if a green light flashed before him, he knew the answer. A commercial supply store would help fund the non-profit.

Gracie glanced toward the old boat next to Ryder's. "Who's that guy? I don't think I've seen him around here, either, and I've lived here most of my life."

Ryder's face grew grim. "I've ministered to him for a while. I see him here now and then. From what I understand, he's made a lot of bad decisions and needs the Lord in his life. I pray for him, and when I get a chance, I provide a little financial help." Ryder rubbed the back of his neck. "But tell me what you're doing in Cranberry Cove."

Blake swallowed hard. Once again, he didn't want to talk about himself. "Oh, I'm taking a little time off work. Trying to make some decisions." A couple of pelicans circled the water before diving beneath the surface, coming up one at a time with fish in their gullet. Were Ryder and Gracie guided by Someone higher? What motivated Ryder to show the old fisherman kindness?

After he and Gracie returned to the car, Blake looked at his beautiful tour guide. "How did you figure out God's plan for your life?"

Gracie clapped her hand over her mouth and laughed. "You don't have an easier question—like what's my favorite dessert?"

Blake grinned. "You and Ryder seem to have a connection with Him."

"Most Christians struggle to understand what God has planned for their lives. God gives us free will to make our own choices, but if we're open to hearing from Him, He'll show us what's best for us." She leaned back on the seat and breathed deeply, a slight smile on her lips.

"God and I aren't best friends, but if He has a plan for me, I'd like to know about it."

After Blake left her off at her house, Gracie unlocked the front door with her key and stepped inside. Mom's car in the driveway meant she'd come home from work a little early. "Hi, Mom."

No answer. Gracie marched from the living room to the kitchen. "You home early?"

From the backyard, Mom took a few faltering steps through the kitchen doorway. She glanced up and startled. "Oh, Gracie." She crumpled a piece of notebook paper in her hand and jammed the wad in her pocket. "I didn't hear you." A frown plastered her face.

Gracie eyed the pocket where Mom had stuffed the paper. "Is everything all right?"

Mom gulped then forced a smile. "I was making a grocery list then decided against going shopping."

In all the years she'd been born, Gracie had never doubted her mother before. Somehow this time she didn't believe the paper in her pocket held a grocery list.

Chapter Four

The next Monday, Gracie dished up the last of the tossed salad in individual bowls and set them in the ample-sized cooler. "Anything else I can do for tonight's meal, Mom?"

"No, honey. Everything else is under control. Don't forget. I'm taking Dad to the Lakewood VA today so we'll be home late. The parttime person James hired will be here later on."

"I'm sure the two of us can handle everything."

A couple of hours after Mom left, Gracie waved at the young college student as he sauntered into the kitchen. "Hey, how's it going?"

The twenty-something guy donned an apron from the hook near the pantry. "Great. I'm pleased Mrs. Mayberry trusts me to work alone."

"Okay, then. I think I'll go home now. You sure you got this?"

He scanned the menus Mom had posted on the bulletin board. "Sure. Have a good evening."

Gracie ambled out of the inn from the kitchen exit and unchained her bike from the bicycle rack. Grateful for an uneventful trip home, she unlocked the front door and stepped inside. A little dusty from cleaning rooms, she headed to her bedroom and showered, changed into shorts and a t-shirt and then strolled toward the kitchen. Her parents would appreciate dinner when they returned. Spaghetti, hamburger casserole?

She flipped on the kitchen light against the approaching twilight then drew her fist to her mouth with a scream.

A cold breeze drifted through the broken kitchen window. The screen rested outside on the ground. Jagged pieces of glass littered the floor. A crumpled, white sheet of paper extended from beneath the saltshaker on the table.

Her hands grew as cold as the brisk wind gusting in, and her stomach soured. The paper hadn't merely landed in that spot. Someone had broken into their home through the window and left the offensive note there.

With an unsteady hand, she picked up the paper and read.

Emma, I'm getting tired of playing games. Those idiots from the casino are hounding me—threatening to kill me. I need that money now. I'm sure you've got connections. And don't go to the police with this. I know how I disgust you. I'll show up at your door and tell everyone in town who I am. Want to see any more of my clever jokes? Then don't ignore this note.

Gracie gagged. Someone threatened her mom. Someone who must know her well since he called her by her first name. Gracie gripped her head with both hands. Mom associating with someone who gambled? Someone who disgusted her? Gracie breathed hard, trying to make sense of the message.

A chill raced her spine. Was Mom's *grocery list* last week connected to the person who broke in today? Or—was the letter's writer the same person Gracie had possibly seen spying on their home? She stepped backward, skidding on a piece of glass, the wall preventing her fall.

She dropped the menacing letter as if the paper were burning hot and covered her face. "Dear God, please protect my family."

The handwritten message threatened her anew. *Call the cops.*

A key turned in the lock.

Had to be her parents. No one else had one. She firmed her jaw and rushed to the front door. She swallowed the gall rising in her throat as she helped wheel Dad's chair into the living room. "You need to come to the kitchen."

Her mother clasped her hands to her cheeks. "What happened?" With faltering steps, she followed Gracie and then gasped. "Oh, no." She slowly picked up the letter and read. Then she lifted her gaze to Gracie. "Are you okay?"

"Yes, just shaken."

Dad's wheelchair squeaked as he propelled into the kitchen and looked from Mom's horrified face to the ominous note still clutched in her hand. "Emma, do you suppose—?"

"No." She glared at Dad.

Dad balled his fists. "If I weren't in this chair, I'd …"

"Honey, please don't say that. It's not your fault." Mom batted at the tears on her cheeks. "I love you more than anything, but… "

If Gracie was to guess, Mom didn't believe he could defend their family.

Dad nodded. "I deserve this. I've done nothing in the last five years to provide for you and Gracie. To offer protection for my family or help pay the bills." He covered his face. "I blame myself."

"No, don't think like that." Mom hugged Dad's neck. She ran her hands up and down her arms and shivered. "In the morning, I'll get someone out to replace the glass."

Gracie pulled her cell from her pocket. "Don't you think we'd better call the police first."

Mom's eyes widened in fear. "No, Gracie. After I explain, you'll know why we can't involve the authorities."

Dad rolled his wheelchair closer to the kitchen table.

Mom gave Dad a quick frown. "There was, uh, someone I once knew who thought I had plenty of money." She glanced at Dad.

Dad nodded.

Gracie was sure Dad knew Mom was having trouble with this man.

"He was a gambler and demanded I help him out." Mom wiped her brow. "Seems he's at it again."

Gracie folded her arms on her chest. "Who, Mom?"

Mom cleared her throat a couple of times. "Oh, just someone I knew a long time ago."

Dad sank lower in the wheelchair and cast his gaze to the kitchen floor.

"Okay, but why don't you want to call the cops?" Gracie shook her head. Mom certainly didn't want to talk about the person.

"Gracie, you must understand. This individual is unscrupulous. He'd turn the whole situation back on me. He'd find a way to get even and jeopardize our whole family." She held her hands out to Gracie. "Please, let's just forget about this."

Gracie slowly turned toward her room, shaking her head. Why didn't Mom want to talk about this person? Then another thought plagued her. Dad understood more than he was willing to say about the mysterious gambler, but why?

Chapter Five

In the inn's dining room, Blake sipped the dark-roasted Columbian breakfast coffee. The nutty taste with herbal overtones had to be the best he'd savored in a while. He set the mug on the table and glanced out the window.

For the hundredth time, he considered Ryder's mention of a fisherman's supply store at the wharf. Was the opportunity a venture he'd like to pursue? The small fishing village of Cranberry Cove, the ambiance of the grand old inn, and the charming wharf with its museum and seafood restaurant drew him. And, he had to admit, so had a certain young woman. Her appeal wasn't merely her lovely red curls and bright blue eyes, but something else. Her connection with God—which he envied.

He pushed away from the cozy table near the window. An omelet with cream cheese and green onions along with a cranberry orange bagel had filled him up.

In the foyer, James Atwood stood behind the freestanding, oak check-in desk and handed two new arrivals a set of skeleton room keys. Not the plastic kind hotels use these days. Another indication of the inn's old-world charm.

Blake rose and zigzagged through the tables, some still occupied, and stopped at the reception area.

James smiled. "Mr. Sloan. How's your stay going?"

"Very well, thanks. I'd like to extend for at least a week. Can I keep my reservation open? I may need to stay longer."

James peered at his computer screen. "Sure. Your room is available." He clicked the mouse a few times and then glanced up. "What brings you to our small community? A vacation?"

Blake shifted from one foot to the other. "I'm taking time off from work." To think about where his life was headed. "I need to complement you on your inn. The food, the service… no wonder the establishment has earned a five-star rating."

James grinned. "My wife actually owns the inn. I work at Pacific Cranberry downtown. I'm filling in for her because we're expecting a baby any minute, and she's on bedrest."

Blake stuck out his hand. "Congratulations, man." He wanted a family one day, but the chances were slim now—at least until he got his life straight.

The beam on James' face couldn't be wider, and he shook Blake's hand. "What do you have planned for today?"

Blake produced his credit card for his bill. "Do you have any suggestions?"

"You could visit my company's cranberry bogs down at the cove. Or mosey downtown to see some of the shops." He ran the credit card through the machine.

"Your employee, Gracie Mayberry, acted as my tour guide yesterday." Blake couldn't help smiling. "We visited the wharf. I was impressed with the foot traffic and the number of boats going in and out."

"We have our share of commercial and private ships." He shuffled a couple of papers into a pile and slid them in a shelf on the check-in stand. "Gracie's father is one of my favorite people. He's a wounded vet, you know."

Blake nodded. "She mentioned him yesterday. I'd like to meet the guy." His stomach did a flip. Mr. Mayberry was exactly the type of military hero he wanted to serve—one who'd given so much to others.

"I'm sure she'd be happy to introduce you." James lifted his index finger as the phone rang.

Blake headed up the staircase to his room on the second floor to find his jacket, this time not stopping at the stained-glass window. The cranberry bogs sounded like a good destination for the morning. Afterall, the town had derived its name from the fruit.

Gracie walked out of the room next to his and strode toward him, a plastic carrier with cleaning equipment dangling on her arm. "Hey there, Blake. Meeting Ryder yesterday was quite an experience. His compassion for the old fisherman is something I usually don't see."

"Same here." He still couldn't put the old guy's face out of his mind when he'd glanced at Gracie and him. Was the man someone he knew from Seattle? He scratched his head.

She started down the stairs. "Well, have a great day."

"Gracie."

She paused at the landing and turned. "Yes?"

"You mentioned your dad yesterday. I don't want to impose, but do you think I could visit him? If nothing else, I'd like to shake his hand and say thank you. I admire veterans who've given so much to their country."

Her lips parted. "I think he'd like that, but let me check."

Gracie raised her brows when Blake helped her into his luxurious late model Mercedes. Not only did she not have an expensive vehicle, she didn't own a car. "When you get into town, take Hillcrest on the right. My house is only a few more blocks." Strange that a businessman from Seattle would want to visit her father. But then he'd said he was interested in the military.

He flashed a glance at her and looked at the road again. "I'm glad your father agreed to see me. Did you say he was wounded in the military?"

"Yes, during a training exercise. He lost both legs below the knees, but he's always willing to talk about his situation." She brushed a strand of hair back. "I need to warn you. He's not always as chipper as Mom and I'd like to see him. He won't be rude, but he may tire easily."

Blake gritted his teeth. "I understand. My grandfather barely escaped enemy fire when he served in the Vietnam war. He speaks about how the Lord spared his life and the stress he suffered. He has a strong relationship with God."

"What about you?" She clamped her mouth shut after she spoke the words. Asking him about his connection with the Lord was too bold. She barely knew Blake.

He smiled. "I'd like to get better acquainted with Him. I've always believed in God, but He seems like a stranger, some entity out in space." He trailed his finger on the hood of the Mercedes as he scooted around and opened her door. If he was turned off by their simple lifestyle, he showed no indication. He gripped her hand and helped her out of the car and onto the sidewalk. With a smile, he looked toward the house.

Gracie opened the gate to the white fence around the perimeter of their home. They walked up the sidewalk to the front door. Now he'd see their modest two-bedroom home which might be a tenth or even a hundredth the size of his. But the love her family shared was more important than opulence. "Come on in. Dad's waiting."

Blake followed Gracie to the door of the cottage, his pulse pounding harder than usual. He held compassion for the man, but ordinarily speaking to a wounded vet wouldn't have impacted him like this. Things had changed.

"Dad," Gracie called as they stepped over the threshold into the small living room. "We're here."

Across the room, a forty-something man rested a phone's handset on the base and rolled his wheelchair toward them. "Another one of those calls, Gracie.

Remind me to ask Mom to cancel our landline phone service."

Gracie shook her head. "Still? I figure whoever was calling would give up by now. Blake, we've been getting hang-up calls now for a month."

Blake frowned. "That's odd. No idea who it could be?"

Gracie shook her head. "Dad, this is Blake Sloan."

Mr. Mayberry stopped near the wood fireplace where flickering flames shot sparks up the chimney. "Nice to meet you, Blake." He reached to give Blake a handshake and then rested his fingers on the blanket covering his lap.

"Thanks for seeing me, sir." A sudden desire to stand at attention and salute almost overcame Blake. Deep within the man's brown eyes, Blake read pain, possibly the result of being confined to a wheelchair, not to speak of the horror he'd endured. The man's shoulders slumped as if he had surrendered all expectations for the future.

"Have a seat, Blake. Gracie tells me you're from Seattle." The wounded veteran waved toward two straight-back chairs.

"Yes, sir. I'm enjoying Cranberry Cove, the salt air, the fresh seafood. I'd like to ask a few questions if you don't mind. I'm interested in the feasibility of beginning a non-profit to aid wounded warriors."

Mr. Mayberry nodded. "Admirable. As it stands now, my wife takes me two hours northeast to Lakewood. We vets didn't ask to wind up like this. But I bet none of us regret serving our country." He gazed at his folded hands.

"I respect anyone who's willing to sacrifice for our

nation." But to what extent did Mr. Mayberry suffer? Was he resigned to life in a wheelchair? Gracie seemed to think so.

Gracie reached for her dad's hand. "Your thinking has changed since you and Mom asked the Lord into your lives, right?"

"I can't deny that." He turned to Blake. "I love the Lord, but He can't use me like this." He threw up his hands.

Blake frowned. He had to help the man somehow. "My grandfather also served."

"So, I'm sure he told you what it means to train for war." Mr. Mayberry shifted in the wheelchair. "Facing death changes a man. Though every day I wish I weren't in this chair, I thank the Lord for my family."

Mr. Mayberry's words warmed Blake's heart. The wounded vet held a share of gratitude toward God. "I bet you've got some stories to tell. I'd love to hear some of them."

For more than an hour, Blake listened to one experience after the other. Flames in the fireplace changed to embers, and out the window, the sun sank lower on the western horizon.

Finally, Blake stretched his arms in front of him and stood. "I don't want to wear you out. Guess I better get going."

"I'll walk you to the door." Gracie stood and headed toward the entrance.

Blake shook the man's hand. "Thank you for the visit. You've helped me figure out a few things." And sparked the desire to help this man find purpose once more. A job? A hobby? And perhaps others like him.

Gracie closed the door and paced alongside Blake to

his car. "You were good for him. I believe the couple of hours you allowed him to talk, he didn't grieve his situation. Merely having someone to listen was medicine—exactly what he needed."

"I'd like that opportunity for other vets, too. That is if I'm able to realize my idea of establishing a DAV center in this area."

"I never thought just talking about his experiences would help him heal."

"I learned a lot today." Then Blake's feet froze to the sidewalk. "Wait." He held his hand out to prevent Gracie from coming any farther. In the waning daylight, he spotted a shadowy figure. "There's someone in that field across from your house. They're looking this way with a pair of binoculars."

Gracie gasped. "I see the blurry outline of a man."

The man dropped the binoculars dangling on a strap around his neck and took off into the forest beyond. The person apparently realized they saw him.

Blake raced across the street, onto the field, and then stopped. Why run among the thick trees? Night was almost upon them. He returned to Gracie standing near his car. "Did you recognize him?"

"No," she shivered. "but something similar happened the other night. I thought I saw someone through my bedroom window but chalked it up to my imagination. Now I'm not so sure." She gripped his hand. "Blake, I'm afraid."

The warmth of Blake's hand calmed a fraction of

the fear welling up inside of Gracie. "We have nothing for anyone to steal. Why would someone want to snoop around our house?"

"You don't have any old boyfriends who might be jealous you've been hanging out with me?" Blake snickered.

"No, not really." She paused, taking in Blake's handsome face. Though she hadn't thought of Blake as a boyfriend, the notion didn't sound too bad right now.

"No high school friends who've stopped by the inn?" Blake frowned.

Gracie raised a brow. "Actually, I remember one guy. His name was Freddy Boswell. He used to stop in at Starbucks when I worked there. He kept pestering me to go out with him. I went to dinner with him once, but that was it."

"A guy you dated one time? Doesn't sound like someone who'd stalk you." Blake's hand on hers and his gray-brown eyes said she had nothing to fear. That he wouldn't let anything happen to her. "Listen, speaking of dinner, let me take you to get your mind off this. I want to try that seafood restaurant near where we met Ryder." He grinned a sweet, boyish smile.

"You mean The Wharf." She could use a distraction. "That sounds like fun. Let me get my purse." Gracie grinned. "I'll tell Dad where I'm going so he won't think I got lost in the front yard."

Outside again, she stepped into Blake's expensive car as he held the door. For one silly moment, she pretended she owned a Mercedes. But in reality, she wouldn't trade her life for any material possession.

Closer to Cranberry Cove's downtown district and the water's edge where fishing boats docked, Blake slowed.

A truck was parked to the right side of the road, and the hood stood open.

"Looks like somebody's in trouble. Let me see if I can help." He stopped behind the truck and got out.

Through the front window, Gracie caught a glimpse of the truck's driver hovering near the open hood. He looked familiar. She closed her eyes and opened them again. Yes, she knew. He was the old fisherman Ryder prayed for yesterday. She stepped out of the car and approached the two men. "Hey, Blake. Can I call for help?"

As if the man had seen a phantom, the old fisherman shuffled back a few steps as he tipped his head to one side. "Listen, I got my mechanic coming in a minute." He turned to race toward the wharf.

Blake scratched the back of his ear. "That was strange. He told me he'd run out of gas, and I offered to take him and his gas can to the service station."

"Did you recognize him?" Gracie stared after the man now running onto his boat. "He was the guy Ryder prayed for."

"I thought he looked familiar." He grasped Gracie's hand as they returned to the car. "Why would he need a mechanic to help him get gas? Makes no sense. There's more going on than he's letting on."

Chapter Six

Like a starving man, Blake devoured the last of the pecan and strawberry waffles on the plate. Mrs. Mayberry's skills in the kitchen were as good as his family's cook at home.

He gazed out the wide dining room windows to the gardens and then to the wooded area beyond. He took a breath. Douglas fir grew tall, like mighty sentinels guarding the inn, not unlike the forest near Gracie's house. Last night, the man with binoculars had watched them. But which one of them—him or Gracie? The incident had happened near her house. Who would want to spy on her? She'd dismissed the possibility of an old boyfriend.

"More coffee, Blake?"

His thoughts returned to the dining room.

Gracie stood next to his table with a carafe of the steaming brew.

He smiled at the attractive woman, her auburn curls now the color of orange blossom honey in the morning light. "Yes, please."

She filled his cup to the brim. "I can't forget about

what happened yesterday."

"Me, either." He pointed to the other chair at the table. "Do you have a minute to talk?"

She nodded and sat opposite him.

Blake lowered his voice. "The old fisherman and his truck had me thinking, but even more strange was the man across the field from your house yesterday. I know you don't think he could be an old boyfriend, but is there anyone who has something against you? Someone who might want revenge?"

Gracie tapped her foot on the wooden floor. "I can't imagine… " She took a deep breath. "Henry Grafton who worked at the library used to ask me a lot of noisy questions every time I went in to check out a book. Did I like to wear dresses or jeans better and what kind of music did I listen to when I was lonely? Then every other utterance out of his mouth was a curse word. I let him know I wasn't interested in him." She sighed.

Blake reached for her hand and wrapped his fingers around hers. "I'm sorry, I don't mean to scare you. I'm trying to reason this out."

She placed her hands in her lap. "I already told you about Freddy Boswell, but he's harmless. He wasn't a creeper, just not my type. I can't imagine he'd spy on me even though I never went out with him again."

Blake swallowed. Not her type? He chuckled under his breath. Was he her type? "You never know about people. You said you also saw someone outside your bedroom window. I think you should make a police report. At least there will be a record of the incidents. The situation could be criminal harassment."

Gracie stepped out of Blake's Mercedes and looked up and down Pacific Avenue. What was she afraid of? Face it. Going to the sheriff's office seemed extreme. But she trusted Blake' advice. She'd avoid telling Mom and Dad, though. At least for now.

Blake held the door to the one story, white stucco building. Inside, a female uniformed officer looked up from her desk. "May I help you?"

Gracie stepped closer to the desk. "I need to make a police report."

The clerk shuffled through some papers. "May I ask what this is about?"

"I'm afraid someone is stalking me." Gracie's chest tightened, cutting off her breath. The words sounded foreign, like another person spoke them. In their quiet town, could someone be after her? She'd always felt safe in Cranberry Cove.

The clerk frowned. "Just a moment. I'll check to see if Deputy McDaniel is available." She walked toward an office in the back, entered, and then shut the door behind her.

Until now, Gracie hadn't entirely thought through the incidents—that someone would actually spy on her. Here in the sheriff's office, policemen with their badges and patrol cars parked outside, the notion became more real.

Blake slipped his arm around her shoulders. "Let's not get too concerned, yet." He lowered his voice. "I'm here for you."

His words soothed like a cup of hot chamomile tea

in front of the fireplace at home. He'd included himself in her problem, and the thoughtfulness seemed nice.

The clerk returned with a hulking man in his mid-fifties. The buttons on his uniform's shirt strained with his bulk, and his pants fit a little too tight near the waist. "Please, come back to my office."

After Gracie explained the two occurrences, Deputy McDaniel set down his pen on the long, yellow pad where he'd taken notes and peered at Blake. "Sir, may I ask how you're involved in this case?"

Blake cleared his throat. "I'm a friend of Gracie's. I also witnessed the second incident."

"Okay." His gaze roamed up and down Blake as if he found him suspicious. "There are many reasons someone might be watching you. Often, a stalker is someone you know or who knows you. Be alert when you're outside your home or traveling to work. Never hesitate to call us. You can make a report online if you need to."

Blake frowned. "I've weighed the possibility the guy is spying on me, but now I'm not sure."

The deputy nodded. "That remains to be seen. Miss Mayberry, this is a small town, and there aren't a lot of places a criminal can hide—if he or she remains in the area. I'll put extra surveillance on your home and dispatch more police cars to your neighborhood."

Gracie nodded. She hadn't told the deputy about her mother's problems because Mom seemed hesitant to do so. Perhaps the extra patrols by her home would end Mom's troubles as well.

Gracie rose from her chair. "Thank you, Deputy."

As she walked out of the office, Blake behind her, she tensed. "I need to get my mind off of stalkers. Do you want to go to the wharf and visit one of the museums?"

Blake guided Gracie with his hand on her back as they strolled from the war museum and onto the wharf's wooden boards. The skies had grayed, and rain seemed imminent. "The First World War Gallery exhibition grabbed my attention." And his heart. "I'll never forget some of the personal stories of the soldiers and their families caught up in the war. Each tale represented a real person."

Gracie nodded, and her curls bounced. "Some of them were hard to read. Like the young soldier who had to leave his fiancé when he got orders for France to fight alongside our allies. There were times when he thought he'd never make it back home, but when he finally did, he discovered his fiancé had died of tuberculosis." A shadow crossed her face. "I can't imagine how he must've felt."

Blake fastened the buttons on his jeans jacket against the drop in temperature. "Those brave people didn't deserve to suffer as they did but voluntarily gave of themselves." He rubbed his forehead. "Like your father." Blake swallowed hard. "I'd like to help your dad and others like him. Do you think he'd listen if I tried to encourage him, maybe even pointed him in the direction of some job possibilities through the VA?"

She stopped and faced him. "For five years now, Mom has tried to coax him to find a job through the VA or somewhere else. If not a job, at least a hobby that would interest him. He shows no enthusiasm for anything. He's not interested in getting prosthetics or increasing his arm strength, even though the VA in Lakewood has encouraged him. Your attention yesterday sparked more enthusiasm than I've seen in quite a while."

Warmth spread in Blake's middle. "I'm grateful." He clasped his hands together. "I'd like to encourage him further. Please pray God will bring it about."

She smiled. "I will, but you can pray and ask God for the same thing."

He'd tried in the past to talk to Him with little success. At least he didn't know whether God heard or not.

A boat docking at the jetty caught Blake's attention. Ryder and his two deck hands, all three in one-piece, waterproof bibs and boots disembarked from the trawler. Ryder waved. "Hey, Blake, Gracie."

Gracie tugged Blake's arm. "Let's talk to him. Mom wants to know what catch he has available this month."

The distinctive aroma of fish, the briny air, and fresh oil swirled around his nose. Screeching seagulls circled overhead.

Ryder said something to the other men and then headed toward him and Gracie.

"Hey, man. How ya doing?" Blake said.

Ryder joined them in front of the museum, and Blake shook his hand.

Gracie brushed a strand of hair off her cheek. "How's your business going?"

"Great. The ocean was calm this morning. We took in a good catch."

Gracie passed a card to Ryder. "Mom would like

you to call the inn when you get some fresh cod." Gracie giggled. "She wants to be the first customer down at the pier when you're set up to sell."

"I'll be happy to. Actually, most of my sales are to the larger companies, but I'm always happy for locals to enjoy some of my catch." Ryder slipped the card in his shirt pocket under the bib of his fishing pants and glanced to his left toward the rundown boat next to his.

Blake squinted in the direction Ryder looked. "Have you talked to the fisherman you spoke with a couple of days ago?"

"Yeah, that same day after you two had gone. He asked a lot of questions about you, Blake. I'm not sure why. Before I thought, I mentioned your name and then regretted it. I'm sorry, man. I avoided giving him any more personal information. Figured it wasn't any of his business."

"No worries. My life isn't a secret, but I don't trust the old guy.

"Ryder, do you know his name?" Gracie said.

"Sure." Ryder looked toward the boat again. "It's Harry Sallow."

Blake sneaked a peek at Gracie to see her reaction.

She stared at Ryder with a blank expression and then frowned. "He's no one I know."

Blake shrugged. "Never heard of him."

Chapter Seven

Gracie set the three plastic bags filled with groceries in the backseat of Mom's car and slammed the door. One more stop—the flower shop for daisies and carnations. Her mother's orders earlier this morning had been to make arrangements for eight tables. "The flowers must come from Cove's Creations in town, and please use the crystal vases from the dining room cabinet," Mom had admonished.

Gracie chuckled. Her mother demanded nothing but the best for the inn. Gracie started down the sidewalk to the floral shop next door.

"Hey, Gracie. How's it going?" A man called behind her.

She turned and peered at him. "Freddy. Freddy Boswell." He'd grown a beard and a heavy mustache since the last time she'd seen him. "How's it going?"

Odd, she and Blake had talked about him only a few days ago. He wasn't as well-groomed as the last time she saw him. He wore baggy jeans and a torn t-shirt, as if he'd thrown on his clothes as an afterthought. How could she have gone out with him even once? Today, his beady eyes and humorless smile turned her off.

He neared her, invading her personal space.

She took a few steps back.

"I wanted to tell you what a good time I had the night we went to dinner at the fish and chips place. You're a good conversationalist."

Insincere flattery if she'd ever heard it. "Thanks, but I need to go. I'm on a mission for my mom." She attempted a smile.

He reached for her hands with his cold, wet ones. "Look, Gracie. I enjoyed meeting your father when I picked you up at your house. I have a connection with him, you know. I did my duty to my country." He lifted his chin. "Four years in the army."

"I remember you talked about it."

"I'd really like to take you to that new restaurant in Oceanview. I heard they have wonderful seafood. Do you think you could make it tomorrow night?"

How to let this guy down easily? She pulled her hands to her side. She didn't want to hurt his feelings. "Thanks, Freddy, but my schedule changes quite a bit at the inn. The owner is off while she has her baby, and they are desperate for the help." Did she sound believable?

"That doesn't seem fair."

She couldn't encourage him but at the same time, she hated to be rude. "Look, Freddy. You're a great guy. I know you'll find a girl who doesn't work like I do." She turned toward the flower shop. "Take care."

Gracie didn't dare look behind her to see his expression. Freddy Boswell wasn't her type and never would be. Especially now that she'd met Blake Sloan. She picked up her pace and took refuge in the cool flower shop that smelled of gardenias and roses.

Two weeks now in Cranberry Cove and Blake hadn't firmed his plans, much less identified possible locations for a business in the area. He edged into his car and drove toward the wharf, yesterday's paper with the ad resting on the passenger seat. His backseat held an umbrella which he'd no doubt have to use given today's cloudy skies.

First, he'd talk to Ryder. At the wharf, he parked and strolled down to the pier. His friend's boat wasn't docked. He'd likely stopped up the coast and would return later in the day with a load of fresh fish.

Blake liked the guy. In fact, he could imagine them becoming good friends. Something about him. As if he felt confident about the direction of his life. Genuine.

"Hey."

Blake rotated to the person with a gravelly voice.

Harry, the old fisherman whom Ryder prayed for and whose truck had broken down, picked up his pace and approached.

"Hey, how ya doing? Did you get gas in your vehicle the other night?" Blake tried to plaster a smile on his face.

Harry raised the left side of his lip in a snarl. "Yeah, what's it to you?"

"Look, I was only trying to help." Strange reaction from the guy. Almost as if Blake had challenged him.

He held a burlap bag in his hand and sauntered closer. His snarl morphed into a grin that sent a chill down Blake's spine. "I been reading about the Sloan Factory Ships in the Seattle papers. You're a wealthy man from what I understand." He slapped Blake's shoulder. "Want to get even wealthier?"

From where had the man picked up information about his family? Surely, he hadn't discovered the family business from the slip Ryder made.

The old guy smirked, and his deep piercing eyes oozed with deception if Blake was any judge of people.

Blake stood to his full height, likely a good five inches over the man. "What are you talking about?"

"Look, I've seen you around the wharf, and I've heard of your father's big-time money-making business. You talk to my friend Ryder. He and I are good buddies." He hmphed.

Blake swallowed the chuckle. According to Ryder's description, Blake figured Ryder didn't see him as a good friend. "Yeah, I've seen your boat parked next to Ryder's. You're Harry Sallow."

Harry swiveled his head left then right as if he feared someone else approached. "Er, yeah. That's me." He held up the burlap bag. "I don't suppose Ryder told you about my lucrative trips up to the Alaska gold mines."

Blake shook his head, restraining the urge to laugh. "No, can't say he did."

"He probably doesn't want to let anyone else in on the action." He glanced at the bag. "Well, here's the proof. Last year when I went up to Fairbanks, I mined for gold and struck it lucky. I've got at least seven pieces of the valuable rocks here." He stepped nearer, his foul breath gagging Blake. Harry lowered his voice. "Look, I ran into a bit of hard times lately. I need to cash out my gold." He slapped Blake's arm and patted the bag. "These gems are worth over $10,000." He cupped his mouth with his hand. "I'll offer them to you for $1000. You can turn right around and sell them for what they're worth or maybe more."

A slow smile crept onto Blake's face. What did the guy take him for? Gold? "Let me see what you've got there."

"If you insist, but you can take my word for it." He reached in the bag and fiddled with something. He looked up, swiped his forehead with his free hand, and glanced down again. A few seconds later he pulled out a couple of nuggets and with a grimy grip, passed them to Blake.

Blake touched the pieces and turned them over in his fingers. Crystals were embedded throughout the rock. He ran his index finger over the sharp edges of the *gold*. "Look, buddy, I know fool's gold when I see it."

Harry grabbed the nuggets from Blake's clutch and frowned. "Naw, look at this one." He dug down deep and pulled out another. "See this fine sample of gold. I'll sell this one for two hundred dollars. Now that's a deal."

Blake shook his head. "I'm sorry, but I wouldn't give you ten dollars for those rocks."

Harry scowled. "You're a stupid man if you think these ain't real. This is your last chance, or I'm walking away."

Blake's patience wore thin. "Find another way of earning an income." He turned and ambled down the pier in the other direction.

"Well, your loss." Harry's words echoed behind Blake.

No doubt Harry was hard up for money, but the *gold*? Did he really think he could convince Blake the rocks were valuable? Was the guy merely down on his luck, or was there more? He couldn't wait to discuss the matter with Ryder.

Blake shook his head and strolled the length of the wharf. An ounce of compassion filled his heart. Harry, no doubt, was desperate, but why? And how did he arrive at that place in life? If Blake had his veteran's service center up and running, maybe he could help this man. That is if Harry was a vet. Perhaps the guy suffered from a mental disorder of some kind.

Blake shrugged and continued down the pier. Toward the end, he spotted the empty building for sale, the one listed in the newspaper. Might be worth looking into for a fishing supply store. He jotted down the name and number of the real estate agent. He wasn't sure what a cash offer would get him, but hopefully he'd have an advantage should he want to buy the building.

On his way back to the parking lot, Ryder's vessel sailed closer to the wharf and slowly pulled in between the pilings of his usual slot.

Good. He waited until the deck hands tied the dock lines before he approached the boat.

Ryder stepped out on the bow and waved. "Hey, Blake. How's it going?"

Blake waved and then grinned. He cupped his mouth. "Request permission to come aboard, sir."

A wide smile on his face, Ryder saluted. "Permission granted. Come on up."

Blake took the ramp and stepped onto the boat. He gave Ryder a high-five. "Did you have a good haul today?"

"Yeah." Ryder's gaze seemed to follow his two men traipsing along the wooden pier. Then they disappeared into a small fish and chips shop. "Seems like I'm docking at Cranberry Cove more frequently now since my client, Ocean Catch, has chosen the Cove for their pickup location."

"You've got a good business going." He patted Ryder's back. "Proud of you, man."

A shadow passed across Ryder's face. "Yeah, but one of these days I'd like to settle down. Maybe find a girl," he laughed, "like the one you found."

"Gracie?" Did it look like they were a couple? "We're just friends."

"Yeah, but I can see the way you look at her, man. Don't tell me it's only friendship."

Blake wasn't ready to talk to Ryder about how he felt toward Gracie. He wasn't completely sure himself. He lifted his finger. "Hey, I want to run something by you. Has our pal Harry ever tried to sell you fool's gold?"

Ryder threw his head back in a laugh. "So, he pulled that on you, too? That old guy is as phony as his gold." Ryder rubbed his forehead. "Though I feel sorry for him, I have a feeling he's always tried to do things the quick and easy way. He's gotten himself in debt and is probably desperate about now."

"I think you're right. I hold more pity for him than anger." Blake bit his lip. If his hunch was correct, the man was up to more than selling fool's gold.

On the way home from work, Gracie maneuvered her bike on the narrow, paved path. She gripped the handlebars and pedaled faster. Home felt more appealing by the minute. From behind her, a motor revved and then slowed. Sweat formed on her forehead and chest. Someone was following her. Her pulse throbbed in her throat. She turned her head to the rear and startled. A truck trailed her not more than five feet away and then sped around and continued down the street.

Was the driver the person stalking her? She'd filed a report. Surely, the police were on the case.

She blew out a stream of air. No, the person in the truck was likely an impatient motorist on his way somewhere.

Though the sun had almost set, the bike path was still visible. One more block and she'd be home.

On the other side of the street, a guy in a dark hoodie glanced up and continued to stare. Straight brown hair protruded from under his ballcap.

She gawked a moment. The person looked a little like Freddy Boswell, but when she'd seen him last week, he'd had a full beard and a mustache. This guy was clean shaven.

He pulled his cap down, rounded the corner, and disappeared. Maybe the individual was the mysterious person she and Blake saw across the street with binoculars. Or the man in the woods.

Gracie's head ached from confusion. She peddled faster, pulled up in front of her house, and then chained her bike to the tree, grabbed her backpack, and rushed inside. If she could finally be free of the potential threats, she'd be happy.

More angry than fearful, she balled her fists. Whoever was stalking her had better leave her alone, or she'd make another police report.

In the kitchen, Mom sat at the table, her head in her hands, and her checkbook and calculator in front of her. She pushed a tear from her cheek.

"Mom. You finished up early today." Gracie rushed to sit in the chair beside her. "What's wrong?"

Mom looked up and forced a smile. "Oh, nothing, dear. I hate paying the bills. That's all."

"I know you better than that. This is about the person trying to extort money from you, isn't it?" She grasped Mom's hand. "Has something else happened?"

More tears welled in Mom's eyes. Sobs wracked her shoulders as she covered her face. "You are so precious. I don't know what I'd do if anything happened to you. I need you to be careful because I can't risk going to the police over this. Not now. I have to find some way to work it out."

"But I don't understand your hesitancy to call the police."

Mom shook her head. "I did once, and let's just say that it didn't turn out well for me. I don't want to go through that again. I was the victim, but his attorney made me look like the criminal, and I almost lost something precious to me."

Gracie leaned her head on her mother's shoulder. She couldn't put more pressure on her. "I'll be extra careful. Don't worry about me."

Her phone rang, and she answered.

"Hey, Gracie, I've got a favor to ask. Would you drive with me to Oceanview tomorrow?" Blake's deep rumble carried over the line. "I want to check out the area and the community college."

"Just a sec. Let me check on something." She lifted a brow and set the phone down. "Mom, it's Blake. Is there anything special going on at the inn tomorrow? Blake wants me to go to Oceanview with him."

Mom gave her a weak smile. "No, honey. You go. The parttime helper's coming in." She opened her checkbook again and perused her calculator.

Gracie nodded and gripped the phone. "Sure. Mom doesn't need me." She could pick up an enrollment application. Signing up for college now might be a pipedream, but at least she had to try.

Chapter Eight

Gracie leaned against the leather seat of Blake's Mercedes and pushed the button to lower the passenger window.

Wet pine needles, ocean air, and campfires brought back memories of childhood when she camped in the state parks with Mom and Dad.

Blake's smile seemed a ray of sunshine lighting the otherwise gray day. His light brown polo shirt brought out the color of his eyes, and his skinny jeans fit his long legs well.

She shrugged. "One day I'll drive you around—that is when I get a car."

He glanced at her, then back to the road and lowered his voice. "I'm happy to drive you anywhere."

Gracie blinked. Was the handsome guy flirting with her?

In Oceanview, Gracie pointed to the turnoff toward campus. "A section of the community college sits on the water. The marine science classes are held on the beach in good weather."

"Nice." Blake turned at the sign indicating the

school a half mile up the road. "Admin office first?"

"Yeah. The deadline for application is getting close."

"Can you apply online?"

"Yes, but call me old fashioned. I want to see those papers in my hand." The application—the first step in reaching her dream. She'd procrastinated, but Blake's enthusiasm about his own plans helped her realize—she could manage a job and school at the same time.

Blake parked in front of a large two-story building. He turned to her, resting his right leg on the seat. "I know you can go after a degree in marine science. I believe in you."

The sparkle in his eyes told her he meant what he said. She believed in him, too. "I'm certain you're in Cranberry Cove for a reason. It's got to be a nudge from the Lord. If I can do anything to help... "

"No woman has ever said those words to me before. I..." He leaned closer and trailed his finger down her cheek.

Though she wanted Blake to take her in his arms, she guessed in front of the admin building at the college wasn't the best location. "I better go in."

He grinned. "Sorry. I shouldn't rush anything between us."

Gracie hoped her smile said she agreed, and she wasn't rejecting him. "I'll only be a few minutes." She rushed inside and walked down the hall to the registrar's office.

The secretary behind the desk smiled. "Yes, may I help you."

Dolphins seemed to be frolicking in Gracie's stomach. "I'd like to pick up an application for enrollment and available scholarships."

"First time enrolling?"

"Yes, I'm excited."

The employee smiled and dug in her desk. "Here you go." She handed Gracie a thick packet.

As if the envelope held a set of keys that opened the door to her future, Gracie's hand quivered as she grasped the manila envelope.

The secretary nodded to a wire rack on the counter. "The applications for scholarships are over there, and you can also access them online. Don't forget to make copies of your diploma and your SAT scores before you return the forms."

Gracie strolled nearer the display to her left and thumbed through the documents. Her hard work and good grades in high school would pay off.

After getting several applications, she held her head high. She marched out of the building and down the sidewalk, papers in hand.

"All set?" Blake eyed her.

She grinned. "Got everything." She relaxed on the passenger seat, opened the packet, and pulled out the school catalogue. Flipping through the colorful brochure, she found the section she wanted to see, the featured classes. "Hmm. Marine biology." Glossy print photos of orca and blue whales, dolphins, and sea turtles sent a tingle to her tummy. "Since I was a kid, sea creatures have fascinated me." She squealed. "I could finish in two years if I went for an associate degree."

"With your enthusiasm, you could do it faster than that." Blake grinned. "What about going to summer school?"

She tapped her cheek. "You're right. No reason I couldn't."

"You want to drive around campus?" Blake said.

"Sure." Gracie turned the page and glanced at the map of campus. "Go left at the corner and circle around to the right."

A group of students in swimsuits, goggles, and fins sat in lawn chairs that faced the ocean. With his back to the water, the instructor swept his arm around from the sea to the class. What was he teaching them? About the winds or ocean current?

"Stop here a moment." She stared at the students and the teacher. "Someday I'll be down there sitting in that class, too."

"I believe you will." Blake's laugh rang through the car.

"Then I'll work at MarineWorld as a trainer." She gripped her hands between her knees. "Maybe even appear in the performances." She laughed. "I just laid out my vision of how my entire life will go."

Blake tapped his head. "I have an idea. If I start a non-profit, maybe we could conduct whale watching tours to raise money. You could act as a guide and narrate the trips—that is when you're not working at MarineWorld."

"Deal." She gave him a fist bump. "Today reminds me of when I was a kid. Mom used to read me the book *The Little Engine That Could.* The engine kept trying to get up the hill and never gave up. I knew then if I tried hard, I could achieve my goals. What could stand in my way now?"

Blake parked in front of Gracie's cottage. The willow tree in front swayed with the breeze. He walked with Gracie past the flowerbeds in bloom with tulips and daffodils.

Gracie patted his shoulder. "You want to come in and say hi to Dad?"

He scratched his head. Would now be a good time to speak to the vet about the idea stewing on his heart? "Sure. There's something I want to discuss with him—if he's agreeable to my proposal."

"If you could encourage him like you did the other day, Mom and I would appreciate it." Gracie frowned, concern written on her face. "I'll be honest. He still sits in his wheelchair and stares out the window every day. I'm more confident than ever he's suffering from some type of the disorder."

Blake followed Gracie up the sidewalk. "Maybe he'll be ready to hear what I have to say. We need to treat him with patience."

Gracie faced him, her brows raised. "Mom and I have been patient for five years."

"I understand." He gripped her shoulder. "I'm hoping he'll listen to someone besides a family member."

"Hopefully." Gracie opened the lock with her key, pushed the door open, and then paused.

Raised voices came from within.

Mr. Mayberry sat beside the window in the rear of the room.

Mrs. Mayberry stood over him with her arms

folded. "Ted, don't you think I want to tell her." Her voice quivered. "I can't. It will only upset her."

Gracie froze, motionless at the door's threshold and stared into the living room.

Mr. Mayberry ran a hand through his hair. "She needs to know, Emma. It's only fair to her—so she'll understand what she's up against."

Blake leaned and whispered in her ear. "Should we come back later."

As if spellbound, Gracie clasped a hand over her mouth.

"Gracie," Blake whispered again and turned her to face him. "This may not be a good moment to visit with your father."

Gracie blinked and peered at him with a gaze that spoke of desperation. "They were talking about me. What didn't they want to tell me?"

Mrs. Mayberry leaned to kiss Mr. Mayberry on the cheek. "Let's pray about what to do. We'll talk more tonight." She headed toward the kitchen.

"Maybe I better go," Blake said.

"No, it's okay. Whatever it is, I want you here." Gracie pulled Blake inside. She walked closer to Mr. Mayberry's chair. "Dad, you got a minute? Blake's here to visit."

Mr. Mayberry, his shoulders slumped, rolled his wheelchair from the window. "How long have you been standing there, Gracie?"

"We, er, just walked in." She flashed a frown at Blake.

Mr. Mayberry held out his hand. "How are you, Blake?"

Blake reached to shake his.

"I'm going to talk to Mom." Gracie paced into the kitchen.

"All right, sweetie." Mr. Mayberry motioned for Blake to sit down. "I appreciate you stopping by to see an old veteran like me."

"Are you kidding? I'm glad you welcomed me in." Blake slid into the chair in front of Mr. Mayberry and leaned forward.

Gracie's father studied his hands in his lap. "I'm glad to see you," he huffed a breath. "I don't have anything else to do." His chuckle sounded like a sardonic laugh.

"That's what I wanted to talk to you about. As you know, I'm interested in serving military veterans."

Mr. Mayberry looked up, dark circles coloring the skin under his eyes.

"I have a dream of one day establishing a DAV branch office in Cranberry Cove. I'd like you to be a part of my plan."

"What?" Mr. Mayberry frowned and threw up his hands. "Are you kidding me?" He swept his palms over his lap. "What good would I do? I'm useless. I don't have legs any longer." He threw off his blanket to reveal two stumps, his limbs missing under his knees. "I'm only half a man."

Blake rose and placed a hand on Mr. Mayberry's shoulder. "I'm sorry, sir. I didn't mean to upset you."

Mr. Mayberry shook his head. "No, I shouldn't have spouted off to you." He took a breath. "Your organization sounds fine, and I wish you luck. Perhaps you can help others, but I wouldn't be of any value to you."

Blake relaxed in the chair again. "You haven't heard

my idea yet. I think you could encourage other veterans and give them hope."

"How?"

"By offering to share your experience with them." Blake bit his lip, not sure how the man would react. "Let me tell you the rest of the plan."

"What? You want me to share with them that day after day, I feel hopeless. That I'm no good to anyone?" He hung his head and swung it side to side. "I'm sorry, Blake. You'll have to find someone else."

Gracie traipsed into the kitchen, not sure what she'd say. Her mother knew something Gracie didn't and figured Gracie shouldn't be privileged to the information.

Mom bent over the sink as she rinsed dishes and then stacked them in the dishwasher.

"Mom, I heard you talking to Dad."

Mom turned to face Gracie, her color fading to white. As if terrified, she gripped her throat. "You— you heard our conversation a few minutes ago?"

"Yes. I'm a grown woman now, not a child. If there's something I need to know, please tell me." Gracie gritted her teeth.

Mom gulped, her eyes darting from one side of the kitchen to the other. "Oh, I… " she coughed. "Your dad and I were talking about our finances. We didn't want to worry you."

Gracie tightened her fists into balls dangling beside her. "I didn't buy that excuse at the inn, and I'm not buying it from you now. This person has you very worried—and the worry is about me. Don't you think I deserve to know why?"

Her mother took a long breath. Mom gripped Gracie's hands. "Your dad and I only want what's best for you. Can you understand that?"

Gracie nodded.

"And I don't believe it is in your best interest to know everything that's going on. I'm your mother. Please trust me to do what's right."

Gracie bit her lip and studied her mother's face. She seemed to have aged in the last couple of days, and Gracie didn't think hiding the truth in Emma Mayberry's best interest. Still, she'd honor her mother in this.

Without a word, she stood and left her mother alone, and doing so tore at Gracie's heart.

Chapter Nine

The next day after the noon meal, Gracie stacked the clean lunch plates in the dining room china cabinet and replaced the tablecloths. She set the small fresh-flower arrangements on each table. Then she bundled the dirty linens and started toward the laundry room.

"Hey, Gracie. You hard at work?"

She whirled around as Blake walked into the dining room. "Mom's got me on kitchen duty today."

He rubbed the back of his neck. "Were you able to talk to you parents last night?"

Gracie set the tablecloths on the chair and stepped nearer. She couldn't tell Blake her mother's secrets. At least not now. "I wish you hadn't overheard the conversation." She glanced at her shoes and up again. "She doesn't want to tell me, and I can't force her."

Blake gripped her shoulder. "I'm here for you, no matter what. Maybe the two of us can get to the bottom of it."

As if she was infused with an extra dose of courage, she smiled at the guy who seemed genuinely interested in her. "I can't thank you enough."

"I give you my word, I won't mention this to anyone, either."

"Thank you, Blake."

"Hey, I came down to say being cooped up in my room is kinda boring. Do you have any suggestions about where to go? It's a gorgeous day."

"Hmm. Wildhorse Mountain Lake is beautiful, and you can drive there. The picnic area is only a fourth mile walk in."

Blake's lower lips protruded, probably trying to make himself look pitiful. He folded his hands in a prayer position in front of his chest. "Do you suppose you could get off and come with me. I'm ready to go crazy." He chuckled. "I need someone to babysit me and make sure I don't get lost."

Gracie laughed and juggled the soiled tablecloths. "Blake Sloan. That sounds like an excuse to me. Mom said I was off when I finish with the dining room." She wanted nothing more than to spend the afternoon with him.

He pulled his elbow down in a victory cheer. "Awesome. Thanks for taking pity on a poor guest." His piteous expression changed to a happy smile.

Gracie carried the tablecloths and set them in the laundry room off the kitchen. She approached Mom who was peeling potatoes at the sink and patted her on the waist.

Mom turned to Gracie. "Honey, please don't worry about last evening. Everything is going to be all right."

Yeah, sure. "Is the kitchen help coming in this afternoon? I'm thinking about riding with Blake up to Wildhorse Mountain. Maybe even take a small picnic lunch." Mom didn't need to know how much Gracie wanted to be with the guy.

Mom gathered the peelings into a pile and gave her a playful grin. "You seem to be spending a lot of time with the young man."

"Mom." Gracie pronounced every letter. "I'm not in high school anymore, you know. I'm old enough to make my own decisions about who I want to hang out with."

"I know, honey. Gotta tease my sweet girl."

Sometimes, jesting was a cover for the truth. In this case, Mom probably wanted to communicate that Gracie should be cautious about people with whom she spent time.

Her mother peeked into the fridge. "Take some of these chicken salad sandwiches and brownies left from lunch. Apples are in the pantry, too."

"Great." Gracie grabbed a basket from the top cabinet and filled the wicker container with the lunch items. She tossed in a couple of bottles of water and then found an old tablecloth to serve as a blanket to sit on. Yet scratching her head didn't help answer the nagging question that popped into her mind. Did Blake want her to go with him as a distraction, or did he actually feel the way she did? He'd said he cared about her, but was he merely caught up in the moment?

Gracie kissed Mom's cheek.

"Drive safely." Mom faced her again, a frown creasing her brow. "I'm so sorry life has gotten in the way the last couple of days."

In the dining room, Blake fiddled with his phone as he sat in the chair near the window.

"All set?" Gracie slipped on her sweater. "Mom gave me a pass."

"Great." He rose from the chair and slid his phone in his jeans pocket. When he smiled, he displayed his straight white teeth.

Gracie matched his pace as they made their way through the living room and to the front entrance.

Blake held the door for her. "I'll drive. You navigate."

"Deal." She piled into the passenger seat as Blake edged into the driver's side. "Especially since you might get lost around here."

"Well." He faked indignation with an upturned chin. He looked both ways as he stopped at the main road.

"Take the road in front of the inn and go east. We'll see the signs for Wildhorse Mountain in about thirty miles."

After a few minutes, he flipped on his Sirius radio channel. "I just remembered something I heard earlier on TV. We've got some early wildfires developing in the southeastern part of the state."

"I didn't hear the report, but we won't have to worry. Wildhorse Mountain lies in the northeastern section. Wildhorse Lake provides a natural barrier from fires in that direction."

Soft jazz played in the car for the next forty-five minutes as Blake maneuvered the winding road up the mountain. They turned at the sign indicating Wildhorse Lake ahead.

"Are you hungry?" Gracie stomach growled. "Let's stop at the campground for a picnic. Those chicken salad sandwiches sound better by the minute."

Blake snickered and parked in the campground's paved lot. "I'm always hungry."

Gracie grabbed the basket and tablecloth from the backseat and then her jacket. "The short drive up here takes us from sea level to over two thousand feet in elevation. Wildhorse Picnic area offers a change in scenery from Cranberry Cove."

Blake laughed. "You sound like a tour guide. Maybe you have a career in the travel industry."

She snickered. "I doubt that. I'm set on a profession in marine science." She pointed to the trail head. "A short walk through the evergreens to Wildhorse Lake."

"Let's go. That lunch basket motivates me." Blake trekked beside her.

Gracie chuckled. "Men—the way to their hearts… "

"What did you say?"

She giggled. "Oh, nothing. You men are all alike."

"Hey." Blake gave her a playful tap and lifted the basket from her arm. "Let me carry that."

After fifteen minutes, the trail opened to a view of the lake shaped in a perfect oval of gentle ripples breaking onto the shoreline.

Blake sucked in his breath. "Love the view. The mountain peaks in the distance are still snowcapped."

Gracie spread the tablecloth under a Douglas fir and patted the space beside her. "Sit down."

Blake lowered to the blanket, leaning against the tree's trunk. "Looking out at the lake feels like I've stepped into another world."

Gracie could remain in the tranquil woods forever if Blake were by her side.

After they finished the sandwiches, fruit, and

brownies, Gracie pulled her knees to her chest and gazed into the distance. "Sometimes I wish I could soak up the beautiful lake, the mountain air, and the forest, and take it all to Cranberry Cove."

"You can." Blake scooted nearer and touched her hand. "In your memory."

He remained next to her as she breathed in the forest-scented air. "If you could go anywhere or do anything in this world, what would you do?"

"Wow. That's a good question. If I tell you, you have to give me your answer, too." Blake's woodsy aftershave quickened her breath.

He smiled down at her. His piercing eyes made her more aware she was a woman. "Sure."

Gracie allowed her mind to explore the concept. "If I could go anywhere, I think I'd choose Israel. To set foot on the land where Jesus walked. To experience the environment where he lived."

Blake lowered his voice. "He's important to you."

"Yes." Her faith journey spilled from her heart before she could stop her words. "As a teen, I became aware of all the wrong I'd done. I knew I needed forgiveness, and there was only One who could do that. I asked Him into my life." She glanced at Blake to see his reaction.

He only studied his hands.

"What about you?"

Blake shrugged. "I believe in God." He swept his hand in front of him. "All this didn't merely appear by chance. I've heard about Jesus in the Bible, but I guess I don't know Him like you do."

Hope built. If she were to guess, Blake Sloan desired a relationship with the Lord. "You can if you'd like."

His silence clued her in. He wasn't ready to talk about the subject. "Your turn to answer the question."

He rubbed the back of his neck and gazed toward the mountains. "Maybe visit a magnificent cathedral in Europe. Surely in those majestic churches I could learn more about God." Blake slid his arm around her shoulders. "I admire your faith, Gracie."

Blake's body next to hers, the warmth from his arm—she couldn't deny the attraction. But there were so many obstacles. She and Blake came from very different lifestyles. And what about his faith? According to his own words, he didn't know the Savior as she did. "Blake." She turned toward him.

Not more than five inches from her face, Blake studied her eyes. "I've never met anyone like you." He leaned closer until his lips hovered over hers.

She pulled him the rest of the way, and his mouth covered hers. Lost in the kiss, she shooed away the doubts from only moments ago.

Blake tightened his arms around her, his embrace was all she knew.

Then he moved away and raked his hand through his hair. "I'm sorry, Gracie. I shouldn't have allowed myself the privilege of kissing you."

She tapped her index finger on his lips. "I encouraged you, remember?"

"I suppose you're right." He brushed a strand of her hair from her cheek. "I'd never take advantage of you though showing you how I feel would be so easy alone up here on this mountain. I respect you too much."

Gracie leaned her head on Blake's shoulder. Though she wouldn't do anything to violate her Christian values, she had to admit to a strong physical attraction to the guy. He became even more appealing because of his integrity—his respect for her rather than thinking of himself.

A spider about the size of a teaspoon walked over her shoe. "Eek." She brushed it off. "I hate spiders."

Blake grinned. "That's just a small harmless creature."

"I know, but I still don't like them." She sniffed. "Wait a minute. Smoke? "Do you smell something burning?"

Blake breathed in and then grasped her hand, lifting her to her feet. "Over there." He pointed into the woods. "Looks like a column of smoke."

Gracie grasped her throat. She'd seen wildfire activity before. "We need to leave now."

Clouds of smoke formed from beyond the trees in the direction of where they parked. She screamed. "What if the flames block an escape, and we can't get to the car and down the mountain in time?"

Blake grabbed the basket and the tablecloth and urged her toward the trail to the parking lot. "Quick."

To their left, two men in orange jackets, one with an axe in his hand, stepped out of the woods. The second guy waved. "Hey, didn't you see the sign? The Washington State Forestry Department is conducting a controlled burn today. The area is off limits."

A flush crept over Gracie's cheeks. "We didn't see the sign."

"The department posted the closure in several newspapers and announced the event on local stations."

Blake stood straight. "My fault. I was driving."

The first man gestured in the direction of the

parking lot. "All right. If you leave now, you shouldn't have a problem getting out of the area."

Finally, in the car, Gracie coughed with the smoke. "I'm sorry. I was the navigator and should've seen the notice. To think instead of a wildfire, we encountered a controlled one."

Blake hacked a few times. "Or maybe I misheard the message this morning on TV. Maybe the announcer said there would be a controlled burn toward the northeast instead of the southeast." He tapped his forehead.

"Well, in any case, we're okay."

He started the ignition and pulled out on the highway. "I guess God looked out for us today. Controlled or not, fire still burns."

Gracie threw her jeans and shirt in the washer, tossed in a laundry pod, and pushed the buttons at the top of the machine. Finally free of the odor of burning bushes and dead leaves, she fell into bed. She took a whiff of a long strand of hair that smelled like fresh peaches instead of fumes—thanks to her hot shower.

She switched out the light and tried not to think of the danger she and Blake had almost suffered. Every muscle in her body ached, and sleep couldn't come soon enough. She took a deep breath and relaxed on the firm mattress. As if floating on water, she drifted off.

A high-pitched squeak like a nail scratching on glass woke her.

Gracie's eyes popped open, and she sat up in bed.

Had she slept and dreamed the sounds outside her window?

She lay down again and pulled the covers to her neck.

No, wait. What if someone was there? She crept out of bed and tiptoed to the window. Pushing the edge of the curtain aside, she peered into the dark night and startled.

A horrid face in a flashlight's beam stared at her from the other side of the window. Evil red eyes gawked from eye sockets under a high forehead and red curly hair. Decaying teeth were surrounded by blood red lips, and—

She held the gaze of the masked fiend, unwilling and unable to turn away.

From behind the disguise, someone blinked and disappeared into the darkness.

Gracie yanked the curtain shut again, chills racing up and down her arms. She opened her bedroom door and ran to the living room, panting. She wouldn't let this person frighten her. She opened the door and stepped outside.

In the distance, a car started, and tires squealed. If she called the police, she'd have to wake her mom and dad, and Mom was already rattled over the person demanding money from her.

A broken window and notes were far different than someone brazen enough to approach her window and simply walk away.

Gracie shivered and hurried inside.

Without turning on the light in the kitchen, Gracie grabbed a bottle of water from the fridge and staggered to her bedroom again.

In bed, her heart beat so hard she felt as if it would explode, and nausea overpowered her. Was the person outside her window connected to the terrible secret Mom and Dad kept to themselves? Before she called the police, she needed to talk to her mother. Something wasn't adding up.

Chapter Ten

Mom slid the pan with the last of her morning crepes from the warming oven and portioned them onto two plates. She spooned berry fruit compote on each and then topped them with whipped cream.

Gracie touched her arm. "Mom, I need a second."

Mom lifted a brow and passed the plates to the college helper James had hired. "Please deliver these to table three." She turned to Gracie. "From your frown, I'd say it's serious."

Gracie nudged her mom away from the dining area and lowered her voice. "Last night, someone looked in my window. Whoever was there left immediately. I checked earlier this morning for footprints or marks on the grass and found none."

Mom gripped Gracie's hand. "Do you think you dreamed you saw someone?"

Gracie shook her head. "I don't think so. The face was all too real. Mom, if this is connected to you, I need to know."

Her mother dropped Gracie's hand, turned her back, and then slowly faced her again. "Gracie, you know your father and I dearly love you more than anything. I've given you my reason for not wanting to involve the police."

"I can read between the lines. I was the something precious you almost lost, but I had to be a young child then. I'm grown now. I can help you."

"God will bring a resolution," Mom whispered.

"Do you think I should make a police report?"

Mom ran a hand over her forehead. "I think—"

"Excuse me, ladies. Do you know if the inn rents bikes?"

Gracie glanced up at Blake. "We have bikes, but they're included in your room fee. We've got a couple in the workroom next to the tool shed. Mom, do you need me for a while?"

"You can leave for the rest of the day. The college helper's here." Mom busied herself at the sink with breakfast dishes.

If Gracie were to guess, her mother was glad their conversation was over.

"Okay, then. Follow me, Blake." She crooked her finger.

Mom glanced up with a look Gracie remembered from childhood when they went to the beach, and Gracie walked out too close to the waves. What was that about? Gracie nibbled the inside of her cheek. Since communication had never been a problem between them in the past, she couldn't imagine why her mother hadn't explained her thoughts or why she appeared concerned. Could it be something about the secret Gracie still believed Mom and Dad held from her?

Blake followed Gracie from the kitchen to the

outbuilding where Gina Price once created her magnificent, stained-glass pictures. She unlocked the door with her set of keys and stepped inside. The two drop-handle bikes with good tires were propped against one wall. "I think these belong to Ashton and James, but they haven't ridden them lately because of the baby."

Blake wiggled the handlebars of the first one and tried out the seat. "Do you want to go for a ride this morning since your mom said you could get off?"

"Yes, I need some fresh air."

"I need a breather, too—after yesterday. I feel bad about upsetting your father. I hope he'll change his mind about helping me out one day—if I can establish the vet center here."

Gracie scratched her head. "He needs to find a purpose for his life. How would you involve him?"

"If your dad can make some changes, like trying prosthetics or discovering a skill that would allow him to earn money, he could share his accomplishments with other vets who feel as he does now, worthless."

"They should listen to him since it's obvious he's undergone the hardships of war."

"No doubt. His injury is proof."

She touched his arm. "There's something I need to say." To tell Blake about last night's incident. "Before we go."

His brows furrowed into a deep V, and he faced her. "Yes, anything."

Her voice squeaked like an unoiled door. "In the middle of the night, a sound at the window awakened me. Someone in an awful mask stared in."

His mouth dropped open. "Did you call the police?"

She hung her head. "No. I didn't want to wake Mom and Dad. I waited until this morning to tell her. She didn't encourage me to notify the police." Again, Mom's troubles were something she wasn't willing to discuss with Blake, but the person at her window was Gracie's problem, not Mom's.

He shook his head. "She could feel as overwhelmed as the rest of us." He grasped her arm. "The deputy said we could make reports online. I think you should now."

She nodded, knowing full well Blake was right. For the next fifteen minutes, she worked on the website and filled out the form. The information said someone would get back with her within twenty-four hours.

Blake walked his bike outside the workshop area. "I'm starting to get worried. Someone is out to scare you, and we need to find who it is."

"Going on a ride today is the best thing I can do. I want to get my mind on something besides stalkers and secrets."

"Let's do it. If any bad guys show up, I'm here to defend you." Blake flexed his bicep and smiled. "Got any ideas about where we could ride? I vote for scenic."

"Are you up for a short ride or a longer, uphill trek?" She locked the door behind them.

"How about the second choice. I always love a challenge." Blake gripped the handlebars and followed her to the side of the inn where she'd parked her bike. "Where did you have in mind?"

"The lighthouse would be a six-mile ride northwest of town toward the ocean. The last half mile, the uphill climb gets strenuous. I've made the trip a couple of times."

"Aww, sounds easy." Blake lifted his chin and

smirked.

Gracie winked. Unless he was in super good shape, the ride would challenge him. "I'll slow down if you can't keep up."

"Ha." His voice bounced off the evergreens across the yard.

They breezed along the road from the inn and into town. Gracie waved at Blake to ride parallel to her along the wide, biker's path through the downtown area.

On the other side of Cranberry Cove, the road began a slight incline. To the right, the sign indicated the turn to the lighthouse.

Gracie cupped her mouth and hollered, "Another mile and we're there." She laughed into the breeze. "But the route's a tough one."

Blake waved her off. "I've got this." A playful grin spread along his lips and lit his face.

Gracie led the way up the winding road to the parking lot marked with cedar logs. Blake's heavy breathing said he'd struggled biking uphill.

Blake propped his bike against a tree and bent to grasp his knees. "Whew." He stood straight and blew out a long breath.

Gracie gave him a high-five. "Good job. You did it."

Blake rubbed his calves and thighs. He blew out another breath. "See… " he huffed. "Told you I could do it." He puffed again.

Gracie pointed to the steel structure near the trailhead. "We can lock them up here and walk the rest of the way." She hopped off the bike and chained the tires to the rack.

Low lying-bushes along the narrow path snagged

her jeans. She stepped around a hole in the dirt path and turned to glance at Blake.

He wiped a drop of sweat from his forehead as he trekked behind her.

Gracie giggled. Though the ride was tougher than biking to work every day, she was probably in better shape than Blake. Afterall, she rode daily.

As if to reward their hard work, the terrain leveled out, and the trees cleared. Near the cliff with the drop-off to the beach below, the lighthouse loomed.

Gracie pointed to the graceful structure before them. "The local tourist attraction. Lighthouses were once valuable sources of navigation—protection from our rocky coastline." A gust of ocean breeze lifted her hair. She brushed the strand from her face, made her way to the cliff's edge, and peered over. "You've got to see this."

Blake shaded his eyes.

Only twenty feet down to the beach below, the waves broke against the rocks, leaving white foam on the sand. Beyond, the silver whitecaps reflected the sun.

"Gracie, this view is incredible. The sea's so quiet." Blake folded his hands under his chin.

She neared Blake, cozying closer to his side. "Ashton told me this is where she and James fell in love."

Blake glanced at her, peered down a moment, and then grinned.

Gracie snickered, giving into her sudden urge to tease. "But then, I guess guys don't think about that kind of stuff."

"Falling in love? Sure, we do, but we generally don't talk to each other about our feelings." Blake stepped closer to her and intertwined his fingers in hers. "I'd enjoy talking about romance with the woman I loved."

Gracie swiped a strand of hair from her eyes. Would she and Blake fall in love one day? Their kiss up in the mountains had thrilled her, and even now his nearness fluttered her stomach. Then she dismissed the thought. They came from two different worlds. She wasn't sure if he walked with the Lord either.

She moved a few steps away and bundled her scarf around her neck against the brisk breeze. Though she didn't want to admit the truth, it was too late. She'd already fallen in love with Blake Sloan.

Blake wrapped his arm around her waist. "Most important right now is making sure you're safe. Did you think of anyone who might be shadowing you?"

She shivered and zipped her jacket. "I still have no idea. The only thing I can figure is whoever is trailing me is the same person Mom won't talk about. The one she thinks it best to hide from me." She gave a sardonic laugh. "For my own good. But I feel that reporting my problems is a step in the right direction."

He frowned. "I don't know your mom as well as you do, but yesterday evening, she undoubtedly had something on her mind when she talked with your dad."

Gracie peered out over the ocean. "Mom has someone who wants money from her." Gracie sighed with the confession. "I thought I shouldn't share her troubles, but they're weighing heavy on me. I can't make up my mind if her problems are associated with mine." She looked to him. "Please don't say anything to her. She's very upset, and she's asked me to leave it up to her. I don't want to add anything to her burden either."

Blake tightened his hold, his touch relieving some of her concern. "I'll do everything in my power to protect you."

The shelter of his arm around her brought security as if everything would be okay. But what if he had to return to Seattle before the mystery was resolved? What would she do then?

"Are you sure you're up to the six-mile ride home?" Blake gave Gracie a playful tap on her shoulder as they headed down the trail to the parking lot. They had gotten lost in the beauty of the landscape and the history of the lighthouse. The sun had begun to lower in the sky.

Gracie hopped onto her bike and started to pedal. "Of course. Race you?"

"You're on." Blake stayed a few feet behind Gracie. "I suggest we get some dinner on the way back to the inn. I'm starved." He couldn't ignore his growling stomach.

She glanced his way and then forward again. "There's a place on the edge of town closer to the inn called Cove Subs and Salads."

"If they have food, I'm game." In town, Blake caught up with Gracie and rode next to her. "I love Cranberry Cove's small-town atmosphere without the busy streets and red lights."

Gracie laughed. "I think we have a total of three lights downtown."

"I can actually see myself living here." The words slipped from his mouth though he hadn't intended to express his thoughts. Face it. He felt comfortable enough to tell the attractive redhead anything.

Gracie lifted from the seat, pumping the pedals harder. "You mentioned opening a supply store for commercial and sport fisherman. Were you serious?"

"I've mulled the concept over for days. Yes." Owning his own business no longer seemed a distant dream but a feasible undertaking. But was Cranberry Cove the right place? He wished God would come down from Heaven, tap him on the shoulder, and provide direction.

The route leveled out. Downtown morphed into neighborhoods as the bike path wound along next to the paved road. The sun had set behind the trees.

A motor gunned, becoming louder by the second. On the opposite side of the street, a dark vehicle veered toward them.

Blake gasped. Headlights and the front fender grew larger. Blake swerved, but the vehicle seemed to follow like a magnet. Blake's front wheel shook as his brain tried to catch up with the consequences if he didn't react in some way. "Gracie, watch out." He swung sharply to the right, shoving her onto the soft grass. Her bike shook out of control. The engine of the vehicle revved. Metal scraped and pain filled his side and traveled up his body.

Gracie screamed.

Blake sailed through the air. He raised his hands to brace his fall and flipped onto his back. A sharp pain gouged his left calf. Warm blood oozed through the rip in his jeans. He held his knee closer to his body and watched the taillights of the vehicle as it sped away.

In seconds, Gracie hovered over him. "Blake, are you okay?"

He groaned. "I... I'm not sure." His leg throbbed with pain. He sucked in a breath.

"I'm calling 9-1-1." She dialed and spoke to the emergency dispatcher. "No, no. I didn't get the license number." She sighed. Would that deter the police? She knelt beside him. "Your cut looks terrible." She pointed to a pile of sharp rocks beside the road. "I'm so sorry you took the brunt of the accident. You saved my life." Her voice quavered. "But I'm afraid it was no accident. The driver intended to run one of us down."

Blake's eyes glazed over, and he moaned. "I think I need to throw up." He grasped his stomach. "But you're safe... "

Gracie peeled the ripped cloth of his jeans farther away from the wound. "You have a deep cut." She tied her scarf around his calf. "This should stop the flow of blood until help gets here."

"Excuse me." A young woman jogged up. "I was running on a side street, and when I came onto this road, I was behind you. I saw the whole thing." She held out a scrap of paper to Gracie. "I got the tag number on the car." She unzipped a pack on her waist and tucked a small notepad and pen inside.

Tears stung Gracie's eyes. "Oh, thank You, God." She stuck the wrinkled note in her pocket.

"I really have to pick up my children from ball

practice, or I'd stay. I included my name and address. I'm so sorry." She glanced at Blake. "I think the car was headed for you, ma'am. This guy saved your life."

That was what Gracie had suspected. Her shoulders tightened and reality hit. She was sure that whoever drove that vehicle was the same person who'd prowled around her house. "I can't thank you enough."

"I'm pretty sure I saw a man in the driver's seat. You have my card. Please keep in touch. I really don't want my kids alone at the park, and I don't have anyone who can pick them up. Please let the police know." The young woman's long blond ponytail swayed as she jogged away.

Gracie dropped to the ground next to Blake and held his hand in hers. "Hold on. The ambulance will be here any minute."

"Where's... the closest ER?" He caught his breath.

"In Oceanview." She tightened her jaw. "I feel terrible that you came to Cranberry Cove only to get involved in my problems." She kissed his forehead. "I don't want anything to happened to you."

"I'll... " he swallowed and then shut his eyes.

After five minutes, a police car followed by an ambulance skidded to a stop on the side of the road. Gracie's stomach knotted into a tight coil as the EMS personnel edged Blake onto a gurney. Finally, the rescue vehicle's taillights disappeared down the road. If she could've taken the blow instead of Blake, she would have.

"Ma'am, we'll need you to make a report." A thirty-something officer pulled out a pad of paper and pen.

Gracie reached in her pocket and passed him the scribbled license number and the card. "A jogger saw it all happen, but she couldn't stay. She said her kids were at practice, and she didn't want them to be left alone at the park. I pray you can find this guy. I've filed a couple of other reports as well."

"Just a minute, please." The policeman returned to his vehicle and appeared to be looking at the computer in his car. After six or seven minutes, he returned. "I saw your reports including the one you made last night. I'll include it in this one."

Gracie outlined the events of this morning as the officer jotted the information down and took pictures of Blake's damaged bike. When he finished, he glanced at her bicycle lying on its side in a clump of grass. "Do you need a ride somewhere?"

She blew out a puff of air. What should she do now? Return to the inn, go to the hospital? She sighed. She needed to get both bikes back to the inn. And she needed a vehicle so that she could get to the hospital, whether or not Blake would be released. "I'll call for a ride so I can take the bikes."

"All right, ma'am. If you're sure. We'll be in touch." He smiled. "Don't worry. With this license number, we should we able to track down the perp."

If nothing else, the officer's words were good news. She dug in her jacket pocket, found her phone again, and dialed the inn.

"The Inn at Cranberry Cove. How may I help you?" James answered.

Gracie breathed a sigh of relief. She could put off alarming her mother. "James." She balled her fists. "There's been an accident. A hit and run at Hillcrest before the turn to the lighthouse. Blake is on the way to the ER."

James heaved a breath of air. "Are you okay?"

In a quavering voice, Gracie explained what happened. "My bike is fine because Blake pushed me out of danger, but he took the car's impact and fell on some sharp rocks. Please don't tell Mom. I'll talk to her when I get back to the inn."

"Don't go anywhere. I'll be right there." He disconnected the call.

The back wheel of Blake's bike was concaved, and the spokes twisted. She shuddered as she imagined what the impact must've felt like. Lowering to the curb, Gracie rested her chin in her hands.

Seven minutes later, James pulled up in his truck. He rushed out of the driver's side and offered her a hand up. His mouth fell open when he spotted the bike Blake had ridden. "Oh, Gracie." He swallowed hard.

After she got in, James lifted the two bikes into the back. In the driver's seat, he turned to her. "I can see why you didn't want me to tell your mom."

"Yes, thanks." She rubbed her forehead.

"Do you have any ideas?" James gripped the steering wheel as they headed toward the inn.

"I'm not sure if Mom told you, but a stalker snooped around our house a couple of times. The incidents were bothersome, yes, but not like today. Someone means to harm either me or Blake. And I don't think it's Blake."

"I wish I had answers— " James lifted his ringing phone to his ear and paused. "Yes. Okay, okay." He gave a quick glance in Gracie's direction. "I'll be right there." He looked to the road again. "I'll be sure to check on Blake when I get to the hospital."

"What?" Gracie grasped her throat. "The hospital?"

He grinned. "Ashton's in labor. I need to get her to

Oceanview General."

"Oh." Gracie clapped her hands and remembered the first time she'd met Ashton at Starbucks. "That's wonderful. Congratulations. I'm grateful I prayed for a healthy delivery earlier this morning. Please don't worry about me right now."

"We'll talk later. If you do see Blake, tell him I came back to the inn, and I should be there soon. I'm praying for him."

James increased his speed for the last few blocks and pulled up in front of the inn.

She hopped out. "Let us hear from you."

James sped off down the road, the bikes bouncing in the back.

Gracie hobbled inside and headed to the kitchen. At the risk of scaring Mom and causing her more concern, Gracie needed to tell her what had happened. "Mom, are you here?"

Mom emerged from the pantry, a bag of flour in her hand. She set the flour on the counter, wiped her hands on her apron, and peered at Gracie. "Oh, honey. What happened? Your face is pale. Something's wrong."

Gracie fell into her arms, a little child again. A stupid move, but her mom's touch soothed the fear. Fear for the next time an assailant might attack—and for Blake. Would he suffer serious repercussions from the impact?

Mom patted her back. "My sweet girl."

After several minutes, Gracie pulled away, and the story spilled out.

Mom shook her head. "I was afraid of this."

Gracie stepped away to see Mom's expression. "What? What were you afraid of?"

Mom wiped her face on a tissue and shook her head, offering no explanation.

No doubt, her mother knew something she wasn't telling, but what was so horrible she couldn't share?

Chapter Eleven

Blake leaned his head back against the ER hospital bed as the doctor prepared to put stitches in his leg.

James had made a hurried visit after leaving his wife in the maternity ward. Though he said he could barely think straight because of the impending birth, he'd call Gracie and ask her to wait for Blake's call. No need for her to come until they released him, and the doc had assured him he would be released. He winced from a needle's prick and then the sting of the medication into the wound.

The doctor looked up at him. "I numbed the area with anesthetics. You should only feel pressure when I close the laceration with sutures. You're lucky the wound didn't go deep enough to injure a bone. The X-ray of your hip didn't show a fracture or break, but you're going to be sore."

Blake took a deep breath. As she'd predicted, he felt the tugs while she worked, but nothing like the sharp, stabbing pain when he'd landed on the rocks.

"Almost finished." She glanced at Blake and back

to her work.

Blake let out a deep breath. "I have a feeling that numbing agent will wear off sooner rather than later."

"I'll give you a prescription for a pain killer, and we'll give you a shot of penicillin." She glanced at him again, this time a frown creasing her forehead. "You said someone ran you off the road while riding a bicycle?"

"Yes. My friend and I went biking up to the lighthouse in Cranberry Cove. On the road back, a dark vehicle crossed the median and sideswiped me." He didn't want to mention the driver was likely targeting Gracie.

"All right, all done." She firmed her lips and faced him. "Mr. Sloan, I strongly advise you to make a police report."

"The police arrived at the scene with the ambulance. I'm sure my friend gave them all the information."

Gracie paced the deck outside the inn, a dull ache running along her leg muscles. But she had nothing to complain about after what Blake suffered.

For three hours, her imagination conjured up the uncomfortable scene. Blake lying on a bed in the ER staring at the white walls, enduring whatever medical procedures the doctors performed. When would his phone call come telling her the doc had released him? That he was ready to return to the inn. James had assured her he was awake and handling the pain.

She shivered and strolled into the yard to the spot

where she'd first met Blake and landed in a puddle. She covered her face with her hands. Though Mom had avoided her questions, she needed to press her for answers.

She circled the yard a few times, her stomach churning. Her ringing phone sent her scrambling in her pocket. "Blake. How are you? What's going on?"

He mostly sounded like the Blake who'd begun the bike adventure with her this morning. "I've got stiches, but the doc's releasing me. I'll need that ride now. Use my car. Go to my room and look in my suitcase. I have an extra set of keys."

She had planned to use her mom's vehicle since Mom worked late tonight preparing breakfast pastries for tomorrow, but she'd do as he requested. "I'll be there as soon as I can. And Blake, I'm so sorry this had to happen." Gracie rushed into the kitchen.

"Don't worry. We'll face this together."

Gracie entered the kitchen, and Mom gave her a half-smile. "Blake's being released. He told me where to find the keys to his car." She gave Mom a quick hug. "I'll see you here or at home."

"Please drive safely." Mom extended her hand to Gracie.

Gracie waved and rushed up the stairs to Blake's room. She turned her master key in the lock and entered. Her heart fluttered with the aroma of his aftershave—like the scent of the forest after a rain. She had to hurry. Couldn't allow him to remain alone at the hospital.

His hard side suitcase sat next to the easy chair. She hoisted the bag on the bed and clicked the locks open. An odd sense of guilt came over her for a second.

Getting into someone's baggage didn't seem right, but then she had to and couldn't tarry. The suitcase was empty except for the keys in a mesh pocket. She hurried out of the inn and to his car.

The elegant ride easily took the turns, and she resisted the impulse to speed. On the other side of town, she turned toward Oceanview. She exhaled. She'd be there in twenty minutes. As she drove up to the ER entrance, she punched Blake's button on her phone. "I'm here. Can I help you to the car?"

"On the way." The wide glass door parted, and someone in scrubs wheeled Blake outside.

Gracie rushed around and opened the passenger door. The sight of the handsome guy seated in a wheelchair—almost like her dad's—tore at her insides. She inhaled but couldn't fill her lungs. She'd had enough of injured men to last her a lifetime.

With a few hops and help from the nurse, Blake relaxed in the passenger seat. He nodded to the other woman and juggled a bag filled with prescriptions and other items. "Bandages, antibiotic ointment, and meds. I got them at the hospital pharmacy."

The sight of Blake, with torn jeans and a bandage covering his lower leg, sent an ache to her heart. She leaned toward him, careful of his wound, and slipped her arms around him. "I'm so sorry. I'll get James to change you to a room on the first floor, so you don't have to climb stairs." She drove from the hospital entrance onto the main road through town. "How is your pain level?"

He patted the bag. "Thankfully, I've got some pain killers."

"Anything I can do, please say so."

"Okay. Did you file a police report at the scene?"

"Yes, and this is good news. I'm not sure if you were aware, but a jogger got the license number. The police should be able to pick up the driver soon. Then this will all be over."

"Oh, yes. I remember someone came over to talk to you. I was on the ground in so much pain all I could think of was going to the ER."

"I'm sorry you had to suffer." She glanced at him and back to the road. "I'm surer now than ever. Whoever is pursuing me, Mom knows something she's not telling."

Blake released a slow breath. "I don't understand. If she does, wouldn't she tell you to protect you?" He shifted on the seat as if uncomfortable.

Gracie slowed for the red light. "I can't imagine why not."

Blake's furrowed brow and dark circles marred the puffy skin under his eyes. He leaned his head back against the leather seat. Silence pervaded the car until she pulled up at the inn.

She slumped in her seat, ready to admit the truth. "The driver was headed for me, and you pushed me to the safety, taking the blow yourself. I'm right, aren't I?"

The next day, Gracie tucked the Egyptian cotton sheet into the mattress, fluffed the down pillows, and placed two pieces of organic dark chocolate wrapped in gold foil on each nightstand. She scrubbed the bathtub until the porcelain shined and then stepped out into the hall. Check. The fifth room she'd cleaned today.

Gracie took the staircase to the first floor and glanced at the old-fashioned grandfather clock in the foyer. Four. Time to help Mom with the evening meal. Her day was almost over.

Stomach rumbling, Gracie paused in the expansive guest living room. She glanced out the window. Maroon, purple, pale yellow, and bright pink tulips adorned the flower beds on the west end of the property.

In the kitchen, the aroma of garlic and tomatoes swirled around her. "Whatcha making, Mom?"

Mom glanced up from chopping tomatoes. "Tonight, I'm serving spaghetti and meatballs, homemade French garlic bread, and tossed salad."

"Any chance I might grab a sample? I missed lunch."

Mom looked up with that motherly smile she reserved for her. "How about the first course for now?" She dished up the leafy salad and took a slice of buttery bread from the warming oven.

"Thanks." Gracie sat down at the kitchen table, bowed her head, and then started in, her stomach happier by the minute. Fifteen minutes later, her salad bowl was empty.

Mom wiped her hands on her apron and sat opposite Gracie. "I hope Blake's doing well. I'm sure he's grateful we've delivered his meals to his room."

Gracie nodded. "I checked on him a couple of times. The wound will heal." But would he be able to put the trauma behind him?

"I've thought a lot about the hit and run incident." Mom shook her head. "I wish you'd ride with me to work. I hate to see you on that bike."

"I don't know, Mom. Who in Cranberry Cove would want to run Blake and me down?" Gracie threw her hands into the air.

"Perhaps someone driving through town."

Gracie shook her head. "Surely one of the workers out at the bogs didn't speed through our neighborhood."

"Those folks are James' employees. I think he's careful about who works for him." Mom fixed her gaze somewhere over Gracie's shoulder. "Surely, he—" Mom snapped her mouth shut.

"What? You have an idea who's behind this, don't you?"

"Honey, let's not talk about it here." She squeezed Gracie's hand. "I love you. I only want you to be careful."

If Gracie didn't know better, she'd think a tear lurked at the corner of Mom's eye.

Chapter Twelve

Wednesday morning three days after the accident, Gracie knocked on Blake's door toting a tray of breakfast. For two long days, she'd yearned to see him.

She hadn't talked to Blake since the college helper had delivered his meals. She had no clarity about the accident, either. Even if Mom had wanted to reveal something about the stalker, an extra trip to the Oceanview market and a plumbing issue at the inn take taken precedence.

"Yeah. Come in." Blake called.

She balanced the tray on one hand and turned the knob with the other.

Blake rested against the bed's headboard, his leg propped on a pillow and a small computer on his lap.

She grinned. "We've got big news around the inn today. Ashton and James have a baby son." She set the tray on the dresser.

Blake smiled. "I'm happy for them. I suppose I'm a bit jealous."

Jealous? He wanted kids, too, no doubt. But with

her? Warmth tickled her insides.

A bag filled with rolls of gauze and bandages lay at the end of the bed. She had to tell him her thoughts if nothing else to ease some of her regret. "I feel awful that you came to Cranberry Cove to relax only to almost get killed."

"I can't see how it was your fault. The injury isn't too bad. No broken bones. Have you heard anything from the police?"

"Not so far. I'd like to call the sheriff's department in a couple of days."

"Couldn't hurt."

Nothing but Blake's recovery seemed important now. "Let me help you change the bandage on your wound." The least she could do for the guy.

"Sure, if you've got a strong stomach." He smirked. "I changed the dressing yesterday. Er... it wasn't pleasant."

She patted his shoulder. "Don't worry. I enjoy helping someone I care about." His injury hurt her almost as much as the cut must've pained him.

He nodded toward the bag of supplies. "I think everything's there."

Gracie peeled the dressing from his bare calf visible under his hiking shorts. She swallowed the shock bubbling up in her throat. The red, raw flesh stitched with sutures glared at her.

"I'm ready... I think." Blake gritted his teeth.

Gracie dabbed the wound with the antiseptic and gauze, trying not to let Blake's sudden intake of air deter her. She patted his arm. "I'm so sorry."

After covering the area with a fresh bandage, she stepped back to survey her work.

"You're the prettiest nurse I've seen in a long time." He gave her a half-smile.

Good thing he didn't know she'd cringed as much as he had. "Not so sure I'm suited for the profession."

Gracie slipped down on the bed next to him, twisting her fingers in her lap. "I'm afraid I'll never be able to thank you enough. You saved my life while risking yours." Allowing the tide of her emotions to rule, gratitude, regret, attraction, she leaned toward him and kissed his rough cheek. "Blake, I… " She couldn't tell him she was falling in love with him. The time was too soon. He might not feel the same about her.

She pulled away. Perhaps she only felt the attachment because of his heroic actions.

Blake reached for her.

She moved and with caution sat up further on the bed.

He pulled her closer and ran his fingers along her neck. "We haven't known each other long, but in these last weeks, I've found I care about you—more than… " He leaned toward her, his lips almost touching hers.

Her pulse raced like she'd ridden her bike to the lighthouse and back again. Only Blake's nearness mattered now.

He searched her face. Then he closed his eyes, his mouth brushing hers.

His ringing phone startled her, and she almost slipped off the bed.

"Ugh. Not the best moment." He glanced at the screen. "It's Dad."

"I'll leave so you can talk." The call likely came at the right time. She had no business kissing Blake in his room.

He smiled and pressed a button on his phone. "Dad, I'd planned to call you."

Blake sighed and pressed the phone to his ear.

"I thought I would've heard from you by now. Where are you anyway?"

Blake supposed he deserved Dad's gruff tone. He should've called sooner. "I'm sorry. I wasn't fair to you and Mom. I'm in a small town south of Seattle on the ocean—Cranberry Cove."

"Hmm. I've heard of the place. It's down near the Oregon border." He paused. "May I ask what you're doing there?"

Blake closed his eyes and rubbed his forehead. How to tell Dad why he came and the events of the last two days. "I've kept something bottled up for the last year."

"What? Son, are you okay?"

"Yes." In a manner of speaking. Blake ignored the pain in his hip and leg and sat up straighter on the bed. "I'm here to figure out some things."

"Well, how long does that take?"

Blake's shoulders drooped. Dad wouldn't be pleased when he told him his thoughts. Could be one reason he hadn't spoken about his ideas before. "After you graduated from college, did you ever think you wanted to work in another profession from Grandpa's?"

"No. The family business is most important."

Blake sighed. No chance now Dad would understand but he had to give it a try. "At least a year ago and before I came to Cranberry Cove, a thought kept coming to me I wanted to be different, to make a living running my own business separate from Sloan." He gulped. "This has nothing to do with the way I feel about you and Mom, of course."

Silence.

Blake's stomach tied into knots, and his wounded leg ached even more. "Please say something."

"If you want the truth... " Dad's voice softened. "There was a time... "

"Yes?" Had he heard his dad correctly? He'd gone through something similar?

"When I first graduated, the idea of becoming a doctor, helping people get well, kindled my interest. But then I figured I might let your grandfather down."

Blake took a breath. "You never told me that."

"Yes, I know." Dad cleared his throat.

"Grandpa would've wanted you to follow your dreams." The same man who encouraged him to do the same.

"Listen, son. Don't get the wrong idea. I'm happy in my role as CEO of Sloan—content with my decision to run the company. I suppose what I'm saying is, I believe I better understand your heart—though I didn't take the time to take it into account before."

Blake relaxed his jaw and unclenched his fist. "You don't know what that means to me."

"Since you've been gone—not having you here, I've done some soul-searching as well."

Warmth spread through Blake's insides. He'd never heard his father speak that way. He could tell him about Gracie now. "There's more. I met a girl here. I believe I'm falling for her."

"Really?" Dad's silence gave Blake no clue as to

what he thought.

"Yes. She could be the one."

Dad laughed. "Follow your heart. That's the only advice I have for you. I love you, son. I want for you what I've always desired, for you to be happy. Come home when you're ready."

"I love you, too." Dad's acceptance lifted part of the burden of the decision Blake had to make. Now if only he and Gracie could discover who shadowed her and why someone wanted to kill her.

"How's Blake feeling?" Mom walked into the kitchen from the deck with her arms full of flowers for the vases in the living room.

Gracie moved from the interior of the laundry area where she folded tablecloths and then to the doorway. "He's okay. I delivered a breakfast tray to his room and helped him change his bandage. He's in good spirits." The accident hadn't detracted from his ability to almost kiss her, either. If his father hadn't called...

"I'm so glad. He must feel isolated here without his family."

"Maybe, but hopefully, we can make him feel at home while he's here."

"When you finish folding, can you please check to see if any of the silver pieces stored in the china cabinet in the dining room need to be polished?"

"Sure, Mom." Gracie piled the last tablecloth on top of the others and stowed them on the shelf with the napkins, table skirts, and placemats. When her phone rang, she looked at the screen. Her heart hammered. The Cranberry Cove Police Department. "Hello."

"Ms. Mayberry, this is Deputy McDaniel."

She walked from the laundry room out the door to the deck. "Yes, sir."

"Do you have a moment?"

She tried to take a deep breath but couldn't. "Yes, of course."

"I think your worries are over. Thanks to the license number provided, we have our culprit."

Gracie gripped her throat with one hand and held the phone with the other.

From the kitchen, Mom glanced toward Gracie and frowned.

"We picked up the suspect last night in Oceanview—Freddy Boswell. He confessed to the hit and run. We have him in custody. Because of his confession and the premeditation of his crime, the judge has denied bail. The psychologist suspects he's unstable. He said he shaved off his beard, but nothing he did could attract your attention."

That explained the clean-shaven stalker last week who looked like Freddy. Gracie tapped her forehead with her palm. "Did he say why he ran over Blake?"

"Jealousy. He was actually after both of you."

"Blake put himself into harm's way to save me." She sighed. As she spoke the words, her heart confirmed what her emotions communicated. She loved him for it.

"We questioned Mr. Boswell regarding the other incidents you reported. From what I gleaned in interrogation, his attention to you turned from adoration to hatred when he realized you weren't interested in him. If the department needs anything more from you, I'll let you know, but for now, you have nothing to be concerned about."

"Thank you, Deputy." Gracie pushed her phone into her pocket again and raced into the kitchen. "Mom, they've arrested Freddy Boswell in connection to the incidents I reported." She gripped her mother's hands.

Mom's face held no expression as she stared at Gracie. As if puzzled, she appeared not to understand what Gracie had said. Then a slow smile crossed her lips. "I'm so glad, dear."

Gracie kissed Mom's cheek and turned to leave the kitchen. She stopped.

While Freddy's actions had been toward Gracie, Mom had someone from her past demanding money from her. Freddy didn't toss the rock and note through their kitchen window. He wouldn't be making demands for money from her mother.

"Is something wrong?" Mom asked.

Gracie didn't turn. "No. I'm okay." She moved to the cabinet to do as Mom had asked. She perused the lovely silver pieces in the china cabinet. Only two needed a touch of silver polish. She took them to the kitchen.

Mom stared out the window, seemingly oblivious to Gracie's presence.

Gracie polished, washed and dried the silver, and returned them back to the cabinet.

Somehow, Gracie had to convince Mom to call the authorities.

Chapter Thirteen

From the inn's kitchen, the blender whirled, sounding like a helicopter taking off. Raspberry smoothies on the breakfast menu, no doubt. Though Gracie had tried since yesterday, now wasn't the right time to speak to Mom. Yet her need to convince her mother to take action against the threats she'd received hadn't gone away. And Gracie's questions would have to go unasked a little longer. Even last night Mom had retired early with a headache, and there hadn't been a chance to talk.

Blake hobbled into the dining room. "Can a guy get a cup of coffee around here?"

Again, the sight of the poor man, limping into the room, and wincing as he sat, touched a place deep inside. He hadn't deserved to be injured. "How about a cheese and bacon omelet to go with it? Mom's breakfast dishes are delicious."

"Yes, please." He sighed.

"The morning paper's on your table." Gracie strode to the sideboard and filled a mug from the carafe then returned. "Cream and sugar are there, too."

"Thank you, Gracie." His expression looked as if he tramped through an arid desert, and she'd offered ice water.

Gracie returned to the kitchen. Doubtful Mom could talk, but she could check. "Blake needs a bacon and cheese omelet."

"Of course. But this one is for table four." Mom turned a fluffy omelet in a stainless-steel pan and then eased it onto the ceramic plate. She added a thick slab of bacon and a twig of parsley. "Please take this to Mr. Ford. And a basket of mixed breads with butter."

Gracie needed to give up for now. No time to confront Mom. What had she been thinking? Gracie delivered the omelet and returned to her post in the kitchen.

At the stove, Mom repeated her omelet-making process—Blake's breakfast.

"Mom, I'd like to talk to you tonight."

A frown creased her mother's forehead, and she glanced toward the floor. "I know, Gracie. Something that should've happened long before now."

Gracie nodded. Maybe there was hope for Mom taking action after all.

Blake's stomach growled again. Who knows? Maybe going to the emergency room and getting stiches made a guy hungry. Or the healing process. All he knew was breakfast couldn't come too soon.

Gracie entered from the kitchen and set a plate with a fluffy omelet in front of him.

"Thanks." He eyed the breadbasket. What would he eat first? A scone, whole wheat toast, a donut, or cinnamon rolls?

"*Bon appetit.*" She grinned and turned toward the kitchen.

Twenty minutes later, the omelet was gone as well as the toast and the donut. Maybe he'd ask to take the cinnamon roll to go. He took another sip of coffee.

"Blake." Gracie returned to his table, an expression he could only describe as relief from her parted lips and smooth forehead. "Can we talk?"

"Of course." He stood and pulled out the chair to his right.

A charming smile spread across her face as she sat down. "I have some good news."

Good news which brought her relief, yet her face didn't look like she believed it. "After the accident, we need something to go right."

"No more concerns about my stalker. He's in jail. No one will run you down the next time you take a bike ride."

Blake exhaled a deep breath. "I don't want to put a name to the jerk, but who is he?"

"Freddy Boswell. I told you about him." She covered his hands with her smaller ones.

Still, the light he expected to see in her eyes wasn't there. "I know you well enough by now. What are you not telling me?"

Gracie tightened her grip on his hands. "Obviously, Freddy isn't the one causing my mother problems. That means someone else out there is worrying her, and she won't tell me who it is."

"I understand. You're trying to be sensitive to her

situation, but you do need to be careful." If Blake knew how to pray, he'd talk to God right now. Gracie, still in danger? He couldn't abide the thought.

After breakfast, Blake returned to his room. If there was anything he could do for Gracie right now, he would. He figured when the cops picked up the stalker, life would return to normal.

The time he'd spent with her meant more than anything he could remember. Gracie's faith in God sparked a yearning in him. One day, he wanted to know her God like she did. But was this the time?

He glanced toward the window. A plaque with a verse from the Bible hung on the wall. "Trust in the Lord with all your heart and lean not on your own understanding. In all your ways submit to Him, and He will make your paths straight."

Blake scrubbed a hand over his mouth. God wanted him to trust in Him, but the second sentence tripped him up. How was he to submit to Someone he didn't know—a Person he'd never spoken to?

He folded his hands like he'd seen TV preachers do. "God, I'm not sure how to talk to You. Can You help me? I want to submit my ways to You."

Blake shuffled toward the window and looked out upon the beautifully landscaped yard. No voice rang in his head. No *hello, Blake. This is God speaking.*

Who could he talk to about God? Gracie was busy in the kitchen.

He picked up the keys and limped into the hall.

In his car, he found a comfortable position for his

left leg and started the ignition.

The fir trees towered on either side of the highway to Cranberry Cove, casting shadows on the road—like his obscured, muddled thoughts. He clicked on the CD player and then turned it off again. Where was he going?

A few miles before town, the idea struck. Ryder talked about God. His friend would answer his questions—that is if he was docked today.

Blake followed the route to the wharf and parked his car. His heart dropped into his shoes. Maybe Ryder wasn't in port.

He lumbered toward the area where the boats lined up at the wharf. A seagull circling overhead cried and the breeze picked up. The wind always blew harder near the ocean.

His painful leg throbbed, and he slowed his steps. Ryder's boat wasn't in its usual spot. His hopes of talking to the guy dissolved.

Straight across, docked in its regular mooring, the old fisherman's boat appeared even more rusted and rundown. What caused people to end up like that guy? Had hard times come his way? Maybe he had a family somewhere but then gave into the temptations of alcohol or drugs? Blake supposed he'd never know.

He hobbled toward the end of the wooden structure past a fish-cleaning station and back again. If he couldn't talk to Ryder now, he'd try another time, maybe in the morning. He glanced up at the sound of an approaching vessel.

Ryder's trawler glided slowly into his space and stopped.

His heart a little lighter, Blake waited for the

crewman to complete the docking process. Then he made his way to the end, walked the wide plank to the ship, and knocked at the cabin door.

After a couple of minutes, Ryder opened the door. "Blake. I thought I heard a knock on my way from the helm. Come in."

Blake limped in and glanced around. The captain's quarters, with the long, leather couch along one wall and the adjacent kitchen space with up-to-date appliances, didn't look much different than the quarters on his father's vessels.

Ryder gave Blake the once over. "Were you limping?"

"Yeah. Long story. Do you have a minute for a chat?" Blake scratched the back of his neck. He'd avoid telling Ryder what happened. Talking about Gracie's situation didn't seem the right thing to do now.

"Sure, buddy. Sit down." Ryder extended his hand to the couch, and he pulled up another chair. "The crewmen left to walk around the dock for a while so we have privacy."

Blake eased onto the couch. He longed to bounce his story off another guy, and Ryder was someone Blake could trust.

For the next half hour, Blake explained how he wound up in Cranberry Cove and the decisions he had to make. "Lately, I've felt a tug… to know God better. I'm aware He exists, and His knowledge is vast. Afterall, he created this earth we're on. I need His direction. I want to know Him like you and Gracie do."

Ryder smiled and rolled his chair nearer. "You're hungry for a connection with God. He says if we draw near to Him, He'll draw near to us."

Ryder's words were like bread for Blake's starving spirit. "Tell me how I can."

"It's simple. Though we've all done wrong, Jesus provided a way for us to have a relationship with God. You see, no one is justified in His sight because He's a holy God. But Jesus, His Son, paid the price for your wrongs—and mine. Tell Him you're sorry for your sinful choices and accept Jesus' gift. I can help you with the words."

Ryder's explanation resonated with Blake. He couldn't deny the times he'd cheated on tests in college and more recently how he'd lied to his dad when he'd neglected to order parts for one of the boats. He'd blamed it on the other company. Then Blake cringed. Once he'd promised his mom and dad he'd wait until marriage for intimacy—not like a lot of people today live. Then he'd spent the night with an old girlfriend and never thought anything about it.

But those convictions were different now—with Gracie in his life.

Yes, he needed forgiveness. Though he didn't understand everything Ryder said, something within whispered that Ryder had answers Blake had sought for years. A knotted mass of confusion unraveled before him. "Yes, I want that."

Blake repeated every word Ryder said. Finally, he lifted his eyes to his friend's. He had no doubt—his life had changed. His leg still throbbed, uncertainty still plagued, but something was different. The change had nothing to do with his feelings, he was sure, but with another part of him that dwelled deep within his heart. For the first time, he felt alive. He couldn't lose the wide grin.

Ryder shook his hand. "You're my brother in Christ now."

"And I didn't even have to go to a grand cathedral to find Him."

"What?" Ryder stared at him.

"I'm joking." Blake clapped Ryder's back. "How can I ever thank you?"

"By telling someone else the good news you heard today."

Ryder rose, shuffled through a drawer in a cabinet across the room, and pulled out a small book. "For you. A Bible. You talked about making decisions. This will be your best source of help."

Blake took a few painful steps toward the cabin door. "I'm going somewhere so I can read."

"Start with the book of John. And don't forget. You can talk to God about anything anywhere."

Did that mean even about him and Gracie?

Chapter Fourteen

That night, Gracie lifted her cold hands toward the orange and yellow flames flickering in the fireplace. She rubbed her palms a few times, trying to ward off the cool evening air, yet the prospect of what loomed ahead chilled her more.

Dad rolled his wheelchair across from her, and mom edged down in the seat by his side. "Gracie." Dad rung his hands in his lap. "Mom and I should've shared this with you weeks ago."

Mom rested her fingers on his. "Ted. Don't put the blame on yourself. You know I asked you not to say anything against your advice." She patted his arm. "Please forgive me."

Gracie's stomach felt like she'd swallowed a brick. "Mom and Dad, tell me what's going on." Gracie cast a gaze toward her mother. "

Dad rolled closer to Gracie and turned to Mom. "You'd better explain."

Mom gripped Gracie's hand. "Let me speak while I still have the courage. I was young and lived in Oceanview. I met a man who said he came to town from Nevada, and I thought I loved him. We married, but the decision was the worst mistake of my life. Not only did he gamble, he drank—a lot and got mean, sometimes violent." She squeezed Gracie's hand. "As you know, when you were one, I had to leave and return to my parents' home in Tacoma. They convinced me to file charges. I did make a complaint, and I filed for divorce because I couldn't bear to think of him hurting you. The problem is that I did those two things very close together. Your father's legal aid attorney went after me, accused me of using you to gain full custody. He argued that because of my actions, I didn't deserve to have custody at all. Your natural father would never care for you. You know that by his absence. Robert Brewer is an evil, evil man, but he isn't very bright." For the first time in a long time, her mother smiled. "That was the only time he beat me, and I was glad for it. He was arrested, and I divorced him. The judge granted me sole custody and allowed your father supervised visitation. He never asked for it. I met your new dad, and the three of us began another life." She breathed in a long breath.

"It's okay, Mom. Go ahead." Gracie understood now why her mother was hesitant to call in the authorities.

"I hadn't heard from your biological father in years. Your dad and I have been very happy. Then one day about three months ago, I was shopping at Hometown Market. Someone came up behind me and said hello. I turned to see your natural father."

Gracie narrowed her eyes. "Did he—"

"He said he was in trouble and that he needed money. I told him we didn't have extra funds. He walked away, and I thought that was the end of it. Then he started leaving notes in the backyard and under the mat in front saying I had to find a way to get him money."

"The day I saw you with that note, and you stuffed it in your pocket... "

"Yes, that was from him."

Dad patted her shoulder again. "We'll face this as a family."

Gracie drew her feet into the chair under her legs as if she needed to protect herself. She braced for Mom's next words.

"You read the note he left the evening he broke the back window. Every day after that, I found another. The day I saw one in my car scared me the most."

Gracie placed her icy hand in Dad's.

"Here's the hardest part, Gracie." Mom seemed to swallow a sob. "He believes Blake is a rich man, and he's seen you around with him. Robert has never changed. He believes that anyone who has more than him is game for the picking. He threatened to bring harm to us if I don't convince Blake to pay him off." Tears rolled down her face. "I hope you understand why I needed to keep the truth from you. I couldn't allow you and Blake to worry."

Gracie jumped from her chair and hugged Mom. "I'm so sorry this has happened to our family. As Dad says, we'll get through this together." She flinched. "I suppose I should tell Blake."

"Not unless you think it's necessary." Mom grasped Gracie's hand. "I'm sorry my mistake all those years ago brought this mess into our lives." She sighed. "The only bright side is I've got you. I wouldn't trade my precious daughter for anything."

"Mom," Gracie whispered, "everyone makes mistakes, but God can use them for good." Gracie returned to her chair. "I still wish you'd agree to report him to the police. You must have the records that show what he did to you. The police will take that seriously."

"You don't know what he's like. If I go to the police, he might do something worse. I don't care if he hurts me, Gracie, but I couldn't bear for him to lay a finger on you, your dad, or anyone that I believe you might be falling in love with."

So, Mom had been watching her with Blake. "Okay, so for now, I won't share his threats with Blake. Only if it's completely necessary."

Gracie awoke early, sleep evading her. Finally, she knew what Mom had held from her, but the knowledge hadn't improved her anxious nerves. To think, her natural father lurked somewhere in the area. But where? Near the bogs, in a sleezy hotel in Oceanview, at the wharf? She shivered. If she never knew, that would be fine.

To make it more hurtful, he obviously cared nothing for Gracie—not that she expected him to. All he wanted was money. But after all these years, wouldn't he have at least asked about his own child when he talked to Mom? Gracie firmed her lips. Fine. She didn't care about him, either—someone she didn't know.

Dad Mayberry was her father, the man who raised her from babyhood. The notion struck. The definition of a parent didn't always mean the individual who birthed you but the person who cared, who provided, who guided you through the years—as Dad Mayberry had.

The sun rose on the eastern horizon as she biked to the inn. Starting the coffee was one thing she could do to help Mom before she arrived.

After the coffee had perked, Gracie relaxed on the deck with a steaming mug and pulled her pocket-sized Bible from her fanny pack. She flipped to Deuteronomy chapter thirty-one verse eight. "He will never leave you or forsake you. Do not be afraid. Do not be discouraged." The verse brought her the hope she needed.

Later, Gracie cleared the last table in the empty dining room. She turned to the touch on her arm.

"Can you talk a moment?"

Blake's eyes blazed with something she could only describe as joy. "Sure thing. I'll take these dishes to the kitchen and meet you on the deck."

He nodded and headed out the dining room door.

Whatever he wanted to tell her, the news must be better than hers of late—hit and run drivers, stalkers, secrets. She placed the breakfast plates in the sink and glanced toward the deck.

Blake pulled a small book out of his jacket, settled in a chair, and then lifted his chin. A small book like she'd read earlier. Was it a Bible? She stepped out onto the deck.

Clouds had gathered, and she strolled nearer, sitting in the chair beside him.

Blake tucked the book in his pocket and stood. He grasped her hand in his large palm. "Walk with me." He glanced toward the sky. "Before rain starts pouring."

For a few minutes, she strolled beside him, enjoying

the feel of his fingers wrapped around hers. A small bench waited near the beds of rose bushes which would produce colorful blooms later in the spring.

Blake drew her next to him on the seat. Whatever he wanted to say had deeply impacted him. His eyes twinkled, and she couldn't be sure, but his face seemed to glow.

"Yesterday, I went to the wharf to see Ryder. I can't explain it, but all I know is I feel different... " he tapped his chest, "inside." His light brown eyes twinkled as if he knew a secret. "He prayed with me to ask Jesus into my life."

Gracie's pulse pounded harder. "Oh, Blake. I can't believe it. That's wonderful." She threw her arms around him and hugged him tight. An answer to her prayers.

For several moments, he remained in her embrace, his arms around her. Finally, they moved apart.

He looked out at the rose bushes. "I've always heard my grandpa speak about God. I listened to his words, but they had no effect—as if he were telling me about when he went to India. I've never been to that country, never experienced life there. The trip sounded interesting, but I only saw the place through his eyes. Now I've experienced God personally."

She kissed his cheek. "You're my brother in Christ no matter what happens. Nothing can change your salvation." She gazed into his eyes that were bright with the joy of new life, and then she sighed. He'd need his new faith if she ever had to tell him about her biological father.

Chapter Fifteen

The next morning, Blake tucked his cell phone in his pocket, donned his leather jacket, and trekked out the inn's front door.

Once outside, he inhaled the fir-scented air. The sun shone brighter today, and colors were more vivid. Emerald bushes, dark moss spreading along the forest floor, new leaves sprouting in hues of lime. He'd become grounded. God dwelled front and center in his heart.

A block from the inn, Blake stopped as a whiff of fresh morning breeze cooled his face. The aroma of evergreens and ocean air reminded him he'd found a home in Cranberry Cove. But first he had to look further into the plans God had for him.

He shoved his hand into his pocket to retrieve his ringing phone. Gracie calling?

Nope. His father. "Hey, Dad. I have something important to tell you."

"Son, Grandpa is back in the hospital," Dad forged forward as if he hadn't heard Blake. "He had another heart attack, and this time the doctors don't have much hope for his survival. You'd better get back here as soon as you can."

Blake's stomach lurched. How many heart attacks could Grandpa withstand? "May I bring my friend, Gracie Mayberry?"

"Yes, of course. I pray your grandfather has enough time to meet her."

"I'm on my way. Soon as I find Gracie."

"Son, what were you planning to tell me?"

"I'll save it for when I see you."

"All right. God speed."

Blake's fingers flew over his phone with the text to Gracie. "Lord, please allow her to answer quickly." He rushed to the inn and up to his room. He stuffed his bag with a few things and looked at his phone. Still no answer from Gracie. A deep breath didn't relieve the building tension in his gut, replacing his earlier tranquility. He typed in the words again and punched send. Maybe if he called... He dialed her number.

The voice mail announced she hadn't picked up. "Gracie, it's me. Please call me immediately." He tapped his forehead. Why didn't he check in the kitchen? Maybe she was working.

He rushed downstairs and raced through the dining room to the kitchen.

Mrs. Mayberry grated carrots at the kitchen's sink.

He halted at the door. "Excuse me."

She shifted toward him and wiped her hands on her apron. "Blake. Can I help you?"

He firmed his jaw. "Have you seen Gracie? It's very important."

She frowned. "I believe she's at home working on her admission paperwork. Have you tried calling?"

"Yes, and I've texted her a couple of times." He shifted from one foot to the other. "No answer. I'd like for her to go to Seattle with me." He paused to clear the emotion from his throat. "My grandfather—he's critical, and I'd like for him to meet Gracie."

Mrs. Mayberry seemed to relax for a moment, and then she touched his shoulder. "Oh, Blake. I'm so sorry. I'm sure Gracie will want to go. Here, let me try."

After Mrs. Mayberry rang Gracie, she shrugged. "I'm not sure why she isn't answering."

Blake studied the hardwood floor, each panel parallel to the next. "If she doesn't answer soon, I may have to go to Seattle without her. I want her to meet him before ... " His lips refused to form the rest of the words.

Mrs. Mayberry's gaze spoke of sympathy. "I'll pray for you both."

"Thank you." Prayer. What he desperately needed right now.

Blake rushed from the kitchen to his car. One more thing to try, and then he'd make the trip alone. The drive to Gracie's house seemed a hundred miles instead of five. At the curb, his phone rang, and he picked up.

"Blake, I'm sorry. I just got your texts. I put my phone on silent when I started working at the kitchen table. Yes, I'll be happy to go with you."

"I'm here, in front of your house."

Blake's unhappy tone pierced Gracie's heart. His grandfather was critically ill. She understood. If her mom or dad were sick, she wouldn't know where to turn. In her bedroom, she grabbed a bag. She raced to the living room and gave Dad a quick kiss. "Please pray for Blake's family."

"You've got it sweetie." Dad squeezed her hand. "Text me when you can."

"I love you." Gracie raced outside.

Blake waited in his car, leaning against the headrest, his eyes closed.

She threw her bag in the back and settled into the passenger seat. "I packed a few things for an overnight stay."

Blake nodded. "I'm glad you decided to come."

Gracie ran her hand over his shoulder. "You were there for me when my family faced danger. Even risked your life for me. I'll do anything I can to support you." Despite what the future held, she owed Blake that much—to return his kindness.

Blake sped around the curves of the winding road until they connected with the interstate. His knuckles turned white as he gripped the steering wheel. "I hope we're in time."

If he wasn't driving, she'd hold him in her arms to comfort him.

After three hours, they arrived at the city limits, and Blake maneuvered the streets to the West Seattle hospital.

They rushed to the entrance of the sprawling building which occupied an entire block. His cold hand gripped hers as they rode the elevator to the fourth floor and then to his grandfather's room. Blake paused at the door and turned to her, grasping both her hands. "Pray with me."

The bare, white hospital walls seemed to close in. Patients surrounding them were ill and some would die. Life didn't last forever. Someday, she'd leave the earth. Knowing the Savior strengthened her. She held tight to his hands.

He bowed his head. "Lord, please spare my grandfather." Blake's voice wavered. "Let me see him one more time and bring him out of this."

Her heart broke for Blake. It wasn't hard to see how much he loved his grandpa.

He lifted his head and then caught his breath. "Let's— " Blake turned his back to her and swiped at his face. Moments later, he faced her again. "Let's go in."

He didn't have to hide his pain from her. His tears made him even more masculine in her opinion. She wanted to tell him, but this wasn't the time.

Inside, an elderly man lay motionless in the bed, tubes running to his nose and arm. If the heart monitor hadn't beeped with his pulse rate, she might think Blake's grandfather had passed, his face so pale.

Blake neared the man and placed his hand on his. "Grandpa, I have someone I want you to meet."

Grandpa's eyes fluttered open, and a weak smile graced his lips. "Blake, my boy." He spoke slowly and in a whisper. "I'm glad... you're here." He coughed. "I can't go to the Father without saying goodbye."

The time was now. "I have something to tell you." He smiled. "Remember when you said I should seek

God about what He wanted me to do? Well, I did. And I asked Jesus into my life." Blake's heart pounded, and he watched Grandpa's face for his reaction.

A weak smile crept across Grandpa's lips. "I'm amazed at how God uses all things for good. He led you to Him down there among the cranberry bogs and saltwater air. Just remember. I'll be with the Lord waiting for you."

Blake brushed another tear that rolled down his cheek. "No. You're not leaving anytime soon. You're going to get better." Yet, he knew he probably didn't speak the truth.

"Son, only the Lord knows the day… and the hour, but I suspect this may be my time."

Blake wanted to stuff his ears. His grandpa no longer on the earth? He couldn't abide the thought.

Grandpa lifted his eyes to Gracie who stood by Blake's side. "Who's this lovely lady?"

"I want you to meet my close friend, Gracie Mayberry." He wanted to tell Grandpa he hoped she'd be his wife someday, but it was too soon. The idea had only occurred to him. He hadn't spoken with Gracie, either.

Grandpa held out his wrinkled hand to Gracie. "I'm so happy to know you, young lady. I pray the Lord will bless yours and Blake's future marriage."

"Grandpa, she's not my fiancé." Yet.

Gracie stepped closer, the softness of her smile saying Grandpa's mistake was okay—that they didn't need to correct him. "It's a blessing to meet you, sir."

Grandpa's gaze bore into Blake's. "You tell that workaholic father of yours that I approve of her." Grandpa winked. "There's a scripture that says a chord of three strands can't be easily broken. Always welcome the Lord into your marriage." As if exhausted, he drew his hand to his side and closed his eyes.

Moments later the heart monitor straight-lined.

Gracie grasped Blake's arm. "Oh, Blake. I think..."

Blake stepped closer and planted a kiss on Grandpa's forehead. "I love you. I'll see you again one day. Goodbye for a while."

Two RNs rushed into the room and over to Grandpa's side. Blake led Gracie to the back of the room. He brushed away the tears he could no longer control and whispered, "He waited for us. I'm so grateful he gave us the chance to say good-bye."

Gracie's arms wrapped around his chest lessoned a small part of the pain. "I thank God I had time to meet him and receive his blessing."

When Dad entered the room, Blake whispered to Gracie. "Let's step out and give my dad some time alone with his father."

In the hall, they found a small couch near the elevators and sat. Blake rested his hands on his knees. "I think my grandfather's blessing was well-timed. He knew he was on his way to the next life, and he'd not have another chance to give it." He leaned to kiss Gracie's lips. "Perhaps his words were prophetic."

Chapter Sixteen

Gracie peered out the angled windows with the vertical blinds. The bedroom room alone in the Sloan's Seattle mansion was probably larger than three guest rooms at The Inn at Cranberry Cove. The view of Puget Sound took her breath away. To think, she'd spend the night here. "Better than driving back in the dark," Blake's father had said. "Stay until after the memorial on Monday."

A door in the elegant bedroom led to a small deck outside and the beautifully landscaped yard. She walked out and caught a breath of cool, salty air. Since the sun hadn't set yet, she had enough daylight to investigate the grounds.

The sight set her pulse pounding yet nothing could soothe the memory of Grandpa Sloan passing and the grief on Blake's face.

She wrapped her arms around her middle and strolled to the edge of the property bordered by a white fence that marked the drop-off to the beach below. She leaned against the railing and gazed out at the horizon. Sea gulls circled over the water. Their urgent cries blended with the rush of the waves splashing onto the shore.

The Sloan property curved with the coastline. Beyond, other estates loomed, no doubt each an architectural masterpiece. She shook her head when the contrast came to mind—the tiny Mayberry dwelling and Blake's family home. She didn't fault the family's wealth; she merely recognized the stark differences.

She sucked in a breath. Could the disparity impact any future relationship they might have?

Though the day remained warm, Gracie shivered. She turned from Puget Sound to wander past terraced flowerbeds and hearty shrubs, walking a little faster to the house. She tapped her cheeks.

Instead of entering the home from her private deck, she went in through the house's main hall. She ran her fingers over the polished wood of a foyer table. What would Mrs. Sloan think if she knew Gracie's cottage didn't have an entryway or a foyer table?

"Did you have a nice walk? I saw you through the windows." Mrs. Sloan arranged fresh yellow roses in a vase on a side table in the adjoining formal living room.

"Yes. Your home is lovely."

"Thank you, dear." She smiled. "Being the wife of the head of a large company has its challenges as well as its benefits."

"I'm sure it does." Gracie twirled a stand of hair around her finger. If Blake asked her to marry him like his grandpa had predicted and decided to take over the company someday, she could be in the same position.

Mrs. Sloan looped her arm in Gracie's. "Walk with me to the kitchen. I need to check with Cook about dinner. We're having cordon blue, steamed potatoes, and fresh asparagus."

A cook? The same profession as her mom. Though Gracie was a few inches taller than Mrs. Sloan, she felt smaller than the confident, wealthy woman. Her face burned.

They strolled past the formal living room down a long hall. In the next room with its coffered ceiling, a formal dining room table set for twelve filled most of the space. From there, they entered another room containing a couch, TV on one wall, wet bar, and easy chairs.

"This is my husband's space when he needs to relax after a difficult day." She patted Gracie's hand. "You know how it is with a businessman who's responsible for a large company."

Words didn't form on her lips. No, she didn't know how it was. And she wasn't sure how to return to her room, either.

Before she could stop her words, curiosity overcame her. "What occupies your days? I suppose keeping up with the house takes a lot of time."

Blake's mother patted Gracie's arm. "I have plenty of help. Two housekeepers in addition to Cook. It provides time for me to participate in my organizations and clubs. One of the expectations for an executive's wife."

A lifestyle foreign to Gracie. "What kind of clubs?"

"Friends of Seniors is one. We take care packages to elderly people who're isolated in their homes and visit them in the hospital."

"Sounds like a valuable use of your time." What else could she say?

Mrs. Sloan nodded. "Then there's my garden club

and art appreciation group. Christmas is my busiest season with the toy drives and angel tree project."

To the left, Mrs. Sloan guided Gracie into a gourmet kitchen with stainless steel appliances, copper pots hanging from the ceiling, a warming table, and an indoor smoker. Gracie caught her breath. If she didn't know better, she'd believe she stood in a restaurant kitchen, better equipped than the inn.

Mrs. Sloan held her hand out to a stout woman in a white coat and chef's hat. "Gracie, this is Mrs. Smith, our cook."

"Er, nice to meet you." Gracie cleared her throat.

Mrs. Smith looked up from chopping asparagus stalks and smiled. "Are you a friend of Blake's?"

"Yes. We met when he arrived in Cranberry Cove and have become friends. I wanted to be by his side when he came to see his grandfather."

Her eyes glazed over as she peered at the wall above Gracie's head. "Our Blake has certainly grown up. I remember when he used to sneak my homemade chocolate chip cookies." Her wide middle shook with laughter. "But I caught him every time."

"It's been a while since my son has tried that." Mrs. Sloan grinned at Gracie.

Gracie snickered. "I haven't seen him stealing cookies at the inn, either."

"The inn?" Mrs. Sloan furrowed her brows.

If Gracie could take back her words, she would. How could she explain she worked as a housekeeper and her mother the cook? "Oh, yes. It's the B and B where Blake stays while in Cranberry Cove."

Thankfully, Mrs. Sloan didn't ask any further questions.

Mrs. Smith straightened her shoulders. "These days Mr. Blake has enough money to buy an entire cookie company." She laughed and pointed to one of several large refrigerators. "The chocolate tortes I prepared for tonight's dessert are almost chilled."

"Will dinner be ready to eat at the usual time?"

"Yes, ma'am." Mrs. Smith returned to the asparagus.

"All right, thank you." Blake's mother led Gracie to the hall again. "If you'll excuse me, dear, I need to call the gardener. He's here four days a week, and I need to make it five. He can't keep up with everything as it stands now."

"See you at dinner." Gracie waved and walked in the direction she envisioned her room to be. Finally, she slumped into the easy chair by the window in her room and glanced around the space which announced the truth. This house, the Sloan's opulent existence, the clubs—a lifestyle foreign to her. Is this what a future with Blake looked like?

After dinner, Blake held Gracie's chair as she arose. "Dad, a moment, please." He gripped his father's shoulder. "Monday at the memorial service, I'd like to say a few words."

Dad nodded. "Sure, son. I'm meeting with your grandfather's pastor this afternoon. I'll be sure to remind him." He rose from his seat. "Yesterday, when I called with the news, you mentioned something you wanted to tell me."

Blake lifted to his full height. "When I stand in front of the podium at Grandpa's service, and I tell the folks at his living facility about how I'll see him again someday, those won't be hollow words. I gave my life to the Lord a few days ago, and I know where I'm going after I leave this world."

"I'm glad." Dad peered at him for more than a moment. "As of late, your mom and I have discussed learning more about God, too. Your grandfather planted a lot of ideas in our heads."

Dad's words offered some encouragement. Blake fought the sadness creeping into his soul. Yes, he'd see Grandpa someday. In his impatience, he didn't want to wait that long, though. He didn't want to believe his grandfather was gone—period. Blake needed him tomorrow and the next day and next year. He mopped another pesky tear from his eye.

Dad clasped a hand on Blake's shoulder. "We all miss him, son. I'm glad you were able to visit with him before … " He took a deep breath. "You, too, Gracie."

Blake slid his arm around Gracie's waist as they left the dining room. "Let's take a walk. I'd like to show you my favorite place when I was a kid."

Her eyes didn't hold the usual sparkle as she turned her face to him. "Sure. I strolled around the property earlier today. The setting is magnificent."

Why didn't the look on her face match her words? Perhaps Grandpa's death grieved her as much as it did him.

Blake led her toward the back of the house and down the slope to the sound. "When I was a kid, I used to come here." He lifted his hand to the water and the skyline of Seattle beyond. "I dreamed of being like my dad, an executive with his fishing business." Yet all that had changed now. The Lord had shown him a different way.

Gracie ran her finger under her eye and turned away.

He grasped her shoulders and moved her to face him. "Is something wrong?"

She wiped the other eye. "No, I'm sorry for your family's loss."

Something deep within, the conflict in her eyes told him there was more, much more that she wasn't saying.

She gripped his hand and led him down the path again. "I need to talk to you."

Closer to the sound, Gracie stopped at the little gazebo that nestled against a row of Evergreen Huckleberry bushes and faced the sound on the other side.

If she didn't get her concerns off her mind, the thoughts would smolder in her heart.

A full basket of purple petunias hung from the gazebo's roof. She nudged Blake beside her on the teak bench.

Blake's eyes grew wide. "Gracie, this sound serious. What's going on."

"Your parents' lifestyle is one hundred eighty from anything I've ever known."

Blake shook his head. "Guys can be dense at times. You'll have to spell it out for me."

The fragrant air boosted her confidence. "I'm saying

I need to ask forgiveness. When I first enjoyed the majestic view of the sound on your property and took your sweet mom's tour of the interior of the house, in my heart, I criticized your parents' way of life." She drew her palms into a prayer position under her chin. "I'm so sorry. I have no right to look at what you have and judge it against my family's possessions."

"Gracie, I didn't realize— "

She placed her index finger on his lips. "No, listen. I was wrong. I kept thinking about how I could never fit in instead of thinking of you and our friendship. I was self-centered."

Blake hovered over her lips and whispered. "Don't say any more. God forgave me for my wrongs. I don't think I need to, but I forgive you—only because you asked."

Gracie moved away. "There's more. Whether you live in Seattle as an executive over a large company or in Cranberry Cove finding your place there, I want to be by your side. I care about you, Blake Sloan—very much."

Blake's gaze swept over her face as he brushed her lips again. Her heart fluttered when he claimed her mouth. This time she didn't protest as she slipped her fingers under his jacket. The warmth of his body made her tingle.

She snuggled her head on his shoulder and sighed. No need for conversation, Gracie sat by his side. For how long, she didn't know.

Chapter Seventeen

The spicey aroma of cumin and chili powder swirled around Gracie's head as she stirred the meat for taco salad. Two days after returning to Cranberry Cove from Seattle, and she hadn't seen Blake—only talked to him on the phone. Settling into her old life hadn't taken long, either. She'd never regret hers and Blake's conversation at the gazebo.

Blake grieved over his grandpa's death, but there was nothing she could do other than listen and pray for him. His pain would heal over time. Her one regret was she never had the opportunity to get to know Grandpa Sloan.

From the living room, Dad called. "Smells wonderful. Can't wait until dinner."

"I hope you like it. Mom should be here in a moment, and we can eat. The chopped salad and grated cheese are ready."

Ten minutes later, Mom walked in the backdoor from the driveway where she usually parked. "Hey, honey. Something smells good. After making meals all day at the inn, it's nice to take a break when I get home."

Gracie kissed Mom's cheek. "I'm happy to. We're eating healthy tonight. Low carb salad."

Mom set her purse on the kitchen counter and trekked into the living room to give Dad a kiss.

Dad. Though he hadn't sought out the VA yet for employment, he seemed happier lately. Blake was good for him.

"Can I do anything for you, Gracie?" Mom walked toward the kitchen table by the back window with the newly replaced glass.

"You sit down and relax."

"I think I will." Instead, Mom stared out into the backyard. "Oh, no. Did you notice that?"

Gracie set her spoon on the stove caddy and took a few steps toward Mom and the window. "What?"

Mom pointed toward the edge of the yard closest to the garage. "My decorative pot of begonias and verbenas is lying sideways, and the flowers are strewn all over the grass." She opened the back door and rushed out.

Gracie turned the heat down on the meat and followed her. How did it happen? As far as she remembered, they hadn't had a storm strong enough to turn over the potted plant.

Using her spade, Mom shoveled the soil that had spilled onto the ground back into the blue ceramic pot she'd finished with green vines.

Gracie retrieved the flowers whose roots were still intact and helped Mom replant them in the container. "I have no idea how this might've happened."

"Me, either." Mom set the pot closer to the house and stared at it. "Unless… no." She shook her head.

Gracie glanced to her left. "Did you open the garage door today? Usually, you park in the drive without going in there."

"No." Mom took faltering steps toward the makeshift storage area.

Chills raced Gracie's arms as she followed her mother. From the look of fear on Mom's face, Gracie suspected something had gone wrong.

At the entrance, Mom stopped, Gracie by her side.

The old freestanding garage had served as a storeroom for as long as they'd lived in the house. Shelves lined all of one wall with Dad's tools he no longer used. The other side held boxes of things Mom had stored for years: Gracie's childhood toys and books, keepsakes Mom couldn't bear to throw away.

In the center of the room, Gracie's old bike leaned against the back wall along with a couple of yard chairs. Next to them, Dad's wheelchair he used five years ago when he'd been released from the hospital, sat at a strange angle. Gracie looked again at the chair. Something was very wrong.

Mom grasped both sides of her head with her hands. "Gracie, no."

Gracie took a few steps into the garage and then discovered why Mom had gasped. The seat on Dad's wheelchair had been slashed.

Mom rushed toward the chair as if in doing so, she could change what happened.

A dizzy wave barreled over Gracie. Mom didn't have to tell her how this had happened. She knew. She grasped Mom's arm, closed the sliding garage door, and led her mother out the side door to the kitchen. "He must be a madman."

Mom sank into the kitchen chair. "He's a desperate man. This is a warning. He's not going to wait much longer for the money."

Gracie embraced her mom. "We need to call the authorities. At least make a police report."

Mom stared at the kitchen wall. "I don't know what to do. I need to think. There must be something that will make him leave us—and Blake—alone. He was unpredictable when we were married, and I think he's more unstable now."

Blake finished the last bite of delicious breakfast waffles and downed his coffee. Though his stomach was happy, concern bugged him after Gracie refilled his mug. A grimace had replaced her usual smile.

Maybe she needed to get away from Cranberry Cove for the day. And he knew the perfect outing for her. Before Grandpa died, Blake had placed a tour of the VA facility on the top of his list. Today would be a good day.

Five minutes later, Gracie arrived to refill his coffee.

"Question. Could you leave early? I'd like to visit the Lakewood VA. I'm on a fact-finding mission." He hoped his smile would cheer her up.

Gracie slipped into the chair across from his. "Actually, that would be great. I need to talk."

Blake covered her hand with his. "I knew something was on your mind."

"You read me pretty well." A slow smile crept to

her lips. "I can leave in an hour."

Gracie lowered the window on Blake's Mercedes and took in a whiff of the lovely forest air. The aroma of wet tree trunks, flowers, and damp moss swirled around her. A sunray bisected a thicket of trees, toying with the shadows and colors on the forest floor. Yesterday's panic faded with every mile.

"I'm happy to see your frown disappear."

She leaned against the headrest. "Getting away today is the medicine I need."

The road wound through tall Douglas fir bordering either side of the highway as she and Blake traveled eastward from the coast. "I've always loved this drive—through Olympia with brief peeks of Puget Sound."

"I take it you've been this way a few times." Blake reached for the dash and switched on soft jazz.

"Yeah, I rode with Mom a few times when she took Dad to Lakewood." She slapped his shoulder. "You brought the right person with you. I know my way around that VA facility."

He drew in a breath. "When a man chooses to serve his country, like with every job, there's the possibility of injury or death. I'm grateful clinics like the Lakewood VA are there to take care of them."

Blake's face, filled with compassion, struck a chord within Gracie. God had blessed him with a heart for wounded vets. She gripped his right hand resting on his leg and closed her eyes. Her biological father cared nothing for soldiers who'd suffered injuries, at least not

Dad Mayberry. To slash the wheelchair of a helpless man… Gracie shuddered. Mom may not want to involve Blake, but he needed to know that they were dealing with a dangerous man.

"Gracie?" Blake glanced at her and back at the road. "Are you okay?"

"No, not really."

Blake frowned.

Farmhouses lined the road now as they neared Olympia and the north-south freeway.

Gracie slipped off her shoes and rested her feet on the seat, wrapping her arms around her knees. How to tell Blake that the rest of the story would impact him as well? Her mouth grew dry. "Mom finally admitted the truth to me."

He inhaled a breath. "What did she say?"

"Of course, you know that this is confidential."

"Gracie, that goes without saying." He sent her a quick smile.

"Mom has received notes demanding money from her. Our window was even broken and a note was left on the kitchen table."

Blake shook his head.

"The worst thing that happened was yesterday. We found Dad's old wheelchair in the garage. The seat was slashed."

Blake turned off the music and pulled to the side of the road. "You've got to be kidding. Who would do something like that?"

"My biological father. He's returned to town."

Blake firmed his lips and said nothing for several minutes.

"I know what you're thinking. Involve the police.

Mom doesn't want to, but I'm asking her to reconsider." Gracie gulped and swallowed her apprehension. It was time... time to tell Blake the rest of the truth. "The story also involves you."

He frowned and stared at her. "I'm listening."

Explaining how her natural father discovered she dated a wealthy man and demanded money was more difficult than she'd imagined. "I'll understand if you want to walk away from my crazy life and return to your home in Seattle. I wouldn't blame you."

Blake held both her hands in his and peered into her eyes. "If the situation was reversed, would you leave me and return to your former life?"

Her eyes grew misty as her throat clogged. He was right. She'd never want to walk away from him despite any hardship. She slowly shook her head.

"Then you have your answer, Gracie Mayberry. I love you."

The first time he said those words—they thrilled her. "I love you more," she whispered.

Chapter Eighteen

At home that evening with her parents, Gracie watched the embers glow in the fireplace. She set the rocking chair in motion and then turned to Dad, his newer wheelchair a few feet away from Mom's straight-backed chair as he gazed at the fire.

Mom still cut his light brown hair in a short, military style accentuating his handsome features. Lately, the defeat and the fear she saw in his eyes had faded, replaced by what she guessed to be determination and optimism. Did she dare hope he was ready to take the next step of getting prosthetics and job training?

"Do you remember when I was little, and we took a drive up to Rainier Mountain?" Gracie giggled like when she was seven.

The corners of Dad's eyes crinkled. "You wanted to stop at every pullout to get a closer look at the waterfalls. I remember how you stuck your little fingers out to catch the mist. You'd always squeal when some of the drops sprayed your face."

Mom chuckled and stoked the fire.

"I loved the times when you and Mom took me to the ocean. I used to watch the sandpipers rummage in the sand for their dinner. They'd scurry toward the shore as each wave broke."

Dad folded his hands in his lap and stared at the fire. "They were wonderful times—with you and Mom."

Gracie stretched and stood. "I'm a little tired after my road trip with Blake. I better turn in." She hugged them then headed toward her room. "I love you both."

The hot shower soothed her arm and leg muscles, and she rubbed on her favorite lavender lotion. Wouldn't be hard to fall asleep tonight. Over and over, she'd dream of Blake saying I love you. She pulled back the covers and crawled into bed.

A thud and a bang brought her out of the murky world of dreams. She sat up straight. What was that sound? Throwing the covers aside, she took a few barefoot steps toward her bedroom door.

Another clang.

Her heart pounded as if trying to escape her body.

She inched the door open, held her breath, and tiptoed into the hall. Whatever was going on, it hadn't awakened Mom and Dad.

The embers in the fireplace were dead, and the living room was illuminated only by the waning moon. No one there.

Her hands became frozen blocks of ice, and she understood. Her natural father was somewhere in the house intending to do them harm. She looked around to find something to defend herself with.

The poker next to the hearth would do. She picked up the piece of wrought iron and readied the pointed end to use as a weapon. She crept closer to the kitchen.

Moaning came from within. *Dear Lord, protect us.*

Her stomach churned, and her hand quivered. She flipped on the light but then couldn't stifle the horrified scream.

Dad Mayberry lay on the floor near his overturned wheelchair.

"Dad." Gracie rushed to him. "Are you okay?"

He groaned and tried to push up with his hands.

Fear scissored through her insides as she surveyed the kitchen. Where was Dad's assailant? An overturned plastic cup and a puddle of water covered the floor near the sink.

"Ted!" Mom rubbed her eyes as she stumbled into the kitchen toward Dad.

Dad sat up. "I feel like an idiot. I tried to get a glass of water. I didn't want to disturb you, Emma."

"Oh, Ted. I took a sleeping pill last night and didn't hear you, but you could've awakened me." Mom righted the wheelchair and pulled it nearer to Dad and then set the brake. "Gracie, get on one side, and I'll take the other. Place your arm under his shoulder—"

"No." Dad shooed them away with a swipe of his hand through the air. "It's time I started doing things for myself." He hoisted up on his stubs then scooted near the chair. He backed up and swung himself upward using both arms.

Mom's mouth fell open. "Ted!"

Dad settled himself in the chair. "My weight training is paying off. I found that maneuver on an internet video."

Mom clapped a hand over her mouth as she stared at him. "So that's what you've been doing with those barbells."

Dad held his hand out to Mom and then to Gracie. "I want things to change. You don't deserve having to cater to me all the time."

Still amazed, Gracie returned to her room. That Dad was taking more interest in getting better elated her.

But what instigated his change of heart? Her natural father's threats? Or maybe Blake's encouragement in asking Dad to participate in his non-profit.

She turned out her light, snuggled into bed, and dozed. Then she awoke. She wiped the warm, damp sweat off her forehead and sat up. Even if her father got in better shape, how safe was he if her biological father decided to pay all of them a visit?

Though Gracie's news today frustrated Blake, her words I love you took much of the sting away. If her natural father came after him, he wouldn't fear him as much as if the man attacked Gracie and her family. Mr. Mayberry couldn't defend them. How would Gracie and Mrs. Mayberry fare against the man?

In the dark room, he opened the blinds at the window and gazed out upon the tree that towered over the previous owner's grave. He'd enjoyed hearing the stories about how Ms. Price had found her true love in Cranberry Cove and about the jewels that were hidden at the inn.

He smiled. Sounded like something women read in a romance novel.

Pulling back the bedsheets, he sniffed. They

smelled like lavender and cloves. Had Gracie made up his room? He crawled under the fresh covers and closed his eyes. The pillow supported the weight of his head.

The breeze cooled him as he and Gracie trekked up the path to the lighthouse. He couldn't actually see the tall structure which protected the coastline, but he knew what loomed ahead. He'd been there before.

The tall Douglas fir, thick along either side of the path, obscured the daylight. He held her hand tighter, his heart pounding. Something didn't feel right.

Finally, the path ended at the break in the trees. Though the sun permeated his skin, he shook with the chill that traversed his body. Danger lurked.

Behind Gracie, a dark figure yanked her hair and dragged her toward the lighthouse and the cliff. The man planned to throw her over the edge. Her scream sent needle pricks down his spine.

He awoke, breathing hard. "It was only a dream," he whispered. Or was it?

Chapter Nineteen

"Great. I'll meet you at the wharf in an hour." Blake disconnected his call with the real estate agent and downed the rest of the coffee in his mug. He'd missed a little sleep last night after his bothersome dream, but it was only a dream. Because his unconscious mind had concocted the delusion didn't mean it would come true.

He clicked the locks on his car, climbed in, and drove to the wharf. Good. Ryder's boat was docked in his usual spot. At the cabin door, he knocked. "Hey Ryder. It's Blake."

Ryder opened the door. "Hey, man. Come in."

Blake scratched the back of his neck. "Would you be interested in checking out an empty building at the end of the wharf? I'm meeting a real estate agent in a few minutes."

"Is this about what I think it is?" A wide smile appeared on his face.

"Yep. I'm looking to purchase the place as a fishing supply store. I'd like your opinion." Merely saying the words sent fireworks to his stomach.

Ryder combed a hand through his hair and plopped on a ball cap that said *Hooked on Jesus.* "You, bet. My business is finished for the day."

They trekked to the end of the wharf, and Blake stopped at the last building. "The storefront would be accessible from here with a parking lot in front and a breezeway along the back. I checked out the specs."

Ryder cupped his hands on the window and peered in. "These sixties-style buildings are old, but from all appearances, the interior looks well maintained."

A middle-aged woman with short brown hair, marched down the wooden walkway toward them. "Mr. Sloan?" A question rang in her voice. Of course, with Ryder here, she wouldn't know which of them had called her.

Blake held his hand out to her. "Blake Sloan. This is Ryder Langston."

She shook Blake's hand and nodded to Ryder. "I'm happy to meet you." She stuck her key in the lock and then indicated they should walk in before her.

"I like the windows in front and these old hardwood floors. The building could work for a fishing supply store," Ryder said. "Very convenient for ocean going vessels as well as town folks."

The agent led them to the backroom. "As you can see, there's plenty of room for a storage area and an employee break room. You actually have a view of the cove here." She indicated the windows running along the back wall.

When Ryder moseyed into the front, Blake lowered his voice. "Would the owner go down on the price if I pay cash?"

The agent lifted her brow. "Possibly. I'll speak to

him, but in any case, you're welcome to make an offer."

"I'll get back to you later on today." Talking it over with his friend seemed a priority.

In the front room, Ryder ran his finger along the wall. "Needs a coat of paint. I'd be happy to help when I'm in port."

Blake couldn't ask for a better friend. "Hey, I might take you up on it."

"All right, gentlemen. I'll lock up when you're ready. Take your time."

After thirty more minutes, Ryder headed toward the door. "Meet me at my boat. I've got some cold drinks in the fridge."

"I'm done looking." Blake turned to the agent. "I have your number. Talk to you soon."

Blake walked with Ryder to his boat.

Ryder pointed to the lawn chairs on the bow. "Have a seat, and I'll get us some colas."

"Thanks." Blake relaxed in the chair and glanced through the window to the couch where he'd sat when he prayed with Ryder.

"Here you go." Ryder handed him a cold bottle of cola.

Blake took a long swig and breathed in a whiff of ocean air. A seagull circled above and settled on a piling protruding from the water.

His friend edged into the chair across from him. "You're serious about settling in Cranberry Cove?"

"I'm surer now than ever that the Lord has sent me to southwestern Washington to serve wounded vets. Seattle, Lakewood, and Bellingham are covered. Yet the vets in the coastal area around Cranberry Cove don't have needed services. I want to open the store first and then venture on with a DAV facility. I plan to leave Cranberry Cove for a few days and return to Seattle to close out business at the office."

Ryder hiked his ankle on his knee. "I admire you, man."

"No, I admire you. You helped me to know the Lord. Asking for His guidance these days feels real. I'm not sure why I didn't depend on Him before."

"I don't know. Maybe you weren't ready. The important thing is you know Him now."

Whether the Lord prompted him or not, Blake wasn't sure, but an idea formed in his mind. "You said you wanted to settle down one of these days. If you did, do you suppose you'd be interested in running a fishing store?"

Ryder stared at him and then broke into a wide smile. "You're serious."

"Yeah. Eventually I'd like to spend most of my time at the DAV office," he threw up his hands, "if I can work it all out."

"Hey, buddy." He grinned. "You let me know when you're ready so I can sell my trawler."

Blake froze, barely comprehending what Ryder said. Then he moved toward him with a smile and a firm handshake. "That's a deal, my friend."

Ryder lifted a brow. "How are things with Gracie, or is it any of my business?"

"I haven't had a chance to tell you, but the cops found the guy who stalked her." He had to keep Gracie's situation concerning her natural father to himself since he'd promised her. It wasn't his story to tell.

A hacking cough in the direction of the boat next to

the trawler caught Blake's attention.

The old fisherman stared toward them, tossed a cigarette into the water, and barked another cough.

Gracie set her plastic carrying caddy with her cleaning supplies in the utility room next to the kitchen's pantry. She glanced down at her stretched and faded t-shirt she'd washed too many times and untied her apron.

Shopping wasn't a priority these days, but she needed a few new things. She glanced at the clock on the wall: 4:00 p.m. The thrift store would be closed by now. Maybe tomorrow.

In the kitchen, Mom prepared the evening meal. The menu posted on the small cork board next to the pantry indicated smoked salmon, Prosciutto wrapped asparagus, and garlic rosemary roasted potatoes. "Wow, Mom. You're outdoing yourself tonight. I think I'll stay for the meal."

Mom glanced up from washing potatoes and smiled.

"I'm actually making spaghetti and meatballs at home. Not as fancy, but the meal will fill our tummies." Gracie found her backpack she'd set in the utility room and attached the straps around her shoulders.

"That sounds wonderful, honey. I'll be home after a while. Oh, can you please bring me the wire bread baskets from the china cabinet before you go."

"Sure." Gracie set her backpack on the floor.

She kissed Gracie's cheek. "Have I told you how valuable you are around here—and to me?"

"Not in a while, but it's good to hear."

In the dining room, Gracie located the baskets in the china cabinet.

"Hey, Gracie." Blake's deep rumble sent a tingle to her insides.

She turned around and smiled. "What are you up to?"

Like a little boy on Christmas morning, he grinned. "I'm meeting a realtor in an hour to make an offer on a building at the wharf."

"Oh, Blake." Gracie squealed. "That means you've decided for sure… "

"To stay in Cranberry Cove? Yes, I'm surer now than ever this is God's will for me."

"This calls for a celebration. Do you want to come to dinner tonight at our house? Of course, it won't be a gourmet meal like Mom's preparing."

"I'd love it—to be with you." He winked. "Walk you to your bike?"

"I'll meet you by the chain-up rack." Gracie dropped off the baskets, secured her backpack again, and left by the kitchen door.

Outside, Blake reached toward her bike spokes. "What's this?" He pulled a small manilla mailer from the front wheel.

"I can't imagine what this is."

Blake stepped closer. "Are you sure you want to open it?"

She hesitated but shrugged. Living life in fear of her biological father was no way to exist. Blake watched as she unhooked the metal clasp and slowly peeked inside. She screamed and dropped the envelope to the ground. "It's—it's—" She drew her arms around her waist and stepped back.

"What?" Blake reached for the envelope.

"Don't!" she squealed. "Don't touch it." A shudder started at the base of her spine and worked its way upward.

A spindle-like leg poked out of the package, as if testing the ground. Then a large brownish spider hurried out.

Gracie jumped back even further.

Blake moved to stomp the creature, but Gracie stopped him. "I'm not a fan of them. They terrify me, but the poor thing has been through enough."

"It's a hobo spider," he said but didn't move against her wishes.

Gracie shuddered again. This time the spider wasn't the reason. Her natural father was a cruel man.

Blake picked up the envelope from the closed end and shook it. Then he turned it over and peered inside. "There's a note."

She cringed. "Will you please look at it for me?"

Blake held the envelope in one hand and a sheet of paper that had been ripped out of some kind of notebook in the other. He perused the piece a moment and then read. "Why do you spend your time cleaning rooms? You could do better than that. Don't you want to live in luxury like your rich boyfriend?" Blake frowned, glanced at her, and down again. "Then you'd have enough money to loan me. Like the spiders? Just saying. Things could get worse."

Gracie's stomach turned to a tangle of knotted ropes. "Oh, Blake." She covered her face but couldn't stop the tears. "He's a monster."

Blake slipped his arms around her and whispered in

her ear. "I'm so sorry."

She pulled away. "No, I'm sorry you had to read that filth." She brushed a tear off her cheek. "Only a few minutes ago, Mom told me how much she appreciates me." Gracie couldn't control her emotions or her voice that had risen to a shrill. "This man has no love or respect for me or my family. How can anyone harbor such contempt for others?" This time, she returned to Blake's arms until her tears subsided.

Blake slipped his arm around her shoulders. "It's difficult to understand, and I can't judge anyone else, but after I gave my life to the Lord, I observed other Christians like Ryder and you. You demonstrate genuine love for others. Treating people kindly whether it benefits you or not. You're unpretentious but grateful for God's provisions." He gazed toward the forest beyond the inn. "There was a time in my life that I believed money defined a man, determined his worth. The people in Cranberry Cove have set me straight. I value the humility I see here."

"I've never known what it feels like to be wealthy, but my heart tells me that a relationship with the Lord far surpasses anything else." She took the envelope from him and crumbled it along with the note into a mutilated ball and tossed them into the dumpster. The ball of trash collided with the bin's inner wall and sank into the smelly garbage.

Chapter Twenty

After dinner and in his room at the inn, Blake's thumb hovered over the number on his phone. He couldn't put if off any longer. It was only fair to his father—and his mom.

A trip to Seattle was fine, but telling his dad he'd made his final decision was another matter. Blake's heart pounded harder when Dad picked up.

"Hey, Blake. Mom and I were just talking about you. How's it going?"

"I'll be home in a few days."

"Really? That's good news. In time for work on Monday morning."

"Not that soon, but Dad—"

"You've made a decision?"

Blake firmed his jaw. "Yes. I know it's sudden, and I should have given you more notice, but I'm anxious to relocate. I'm only driving up to clear out my desk and take care of any unfinished business. I can help you hire my replacement—train him or her if you'd like. Dad, Cranberry Cove is where God is leading me."

Dad cleared his throat. "God is very real to you,

isn't He?"

Blake strolled to the window. In the western horizon, the sun slowly disappeared. "A lot has changed since I first arrived at the Cove. Including a relationship with the Lord. He's more real than ever now. Just as real as he was to Grandpa."

Silence again then a soft chuckle met his ear. "Son, you'll be surprised to know Mom and I went to church last Sunday. We've talked about how worship attendance has been sorely lacking in our lives."

Blake felt like he floated on air. "That's awesome, Dad." *Thank you, Lord.* God had no doubt touched his parents' lives as well.

"So, tell me about your new business venture."

"I'm opening a fishing supply store. I may have to cash in a mutual fund account, but I'll put the money to work in a solid investment."

"Are you sure this is what you want?"

"More than anything."

"There is one thing, though."

"Yeah?" Blake couldn't imagine what Dad would say. Maybe he wanted Blake to work for a month or two—or a year before he settled in Cranberry Cove? His mouth grew dry.

"I'll let you go without your two-week notice, and I'll even train your replacement, but you have to promise me one thing."

What a sweetheart deal. Blake smiled. "What's that?"

"After you marry that pretty lady and have babies, you have to promise to bring them to visit Mom and me."

Blake threw his head back in a laugh. "I believe I

can arrange that."

"When do you suppose you'll propose to her?"

"I'm not sure." The thought whirled in Blake's head faster than the wheels on his Mercedes. He had no idea how to do it. In the movies, he'd seen the guy on his knees showing the woman a ring, but he needed to figure out a special occasion for the moment. "How did you propose?"

"Before I married your mom, she was an airline stewardess. When I asked her to marry me, I took her to the top of the Space Needle for a candlelight dinner. She'd always said she loved her sky-high proposal."

"You thought of something that related to Mom's interests."

"Yeah."

The impression flashed into Blake's brain as if he'd seen a guy actually proposing to his girl. "Thanks, Dad. You gave me a great idea."

The next day, Blake drove down the Mayberry's street, honeybees buzzing in his stomach. But he had to take the next step, to honor Gracie with the old-fashioned custom.

He knocked on the door and wiped beads of sweat from his forehead. First time for everything.

After several minutes, the door swung open. "Blake." Mr. Mayberry reached up from his wheelchair to shake his hand. "Come in."

"I suppose I should've called first, but I need to speak to you."

Mr. Mayberry wheeled from the entrance and motioned toward the living room. "I have an inkling what this is about."

Blake couldn't hide his grin. "Yes, and I also want to talk with you about my non-profit. I have a few considerations for you."

Seated across from Mr. Mayberry, Blake cleared his throat. "I'm in love with Gracie. I'd like to spend the rest of my life with her."

Mr. Mayberry nodded. A look of amusement crept over his face. "I kind of got that idea."

"That's my first reason for showing up today. I need your approval before I propose."

Mr. Mayberry's grin filled his face. "No way I wouldn't approve—after all you've done for our family. Gracie's mentioned your faith in God. He's a part of our lives as well."

"I can guarantee you He's in mine. I'm so thankful to you for accepting me into your family." The first step in Gracie becoming his wife had gone well. He prayed the proposal would, too. Blake propped his ankle over his knee. "Are you still thinking of making some changes—getting prosthetics or perhaps a job?" He trusted the man would be open to his ideas.

"Yes. Before I met you, there was no way I would've considered these possibilities, but, Blake, you've helped me see there is hope, if we trust in God. Circumstances don't need to hold us down." He shifted in the wheelchair. "I know. That's a far cry from my attitude when we first met."

Blake smiled. "That's the second-best news I've heard today. The first is your permission to marry Gracie."

Mr. Mayberry chucked. "I'm determined to shed this chair. I realize it will take time, but I want to be able to walk across this room and back one day. Maybe walk Gracie down the aisle. I've read where amputees can do things like running or skiing."

Blake held up his palm in a stop position. "Whoa. Let's take one thing at a time." His mind raced with more options for the disabled vet. "Once you have your prosthetics, I'd like for you to reconsider my offer of a job in my Cranberry Cove office."

"I remember when you mentioned it before, but specifically what do you envision that I would do?" Mr. Mayberry scratched his head.

"I believe you'd make a great resource to the discouraged veteran who believes he has no hope. Maybe share your story. I've heard it said that another person can't truly understand what you're going through unless the person has experienced it, too. Those men or women are going to listen to you. But that is only part of what goes on in a DAV office. We'll both learn more together."

Mr. Mayberry's face radiated with anticipation. "I'm sorry about the way I behaved last time you spoke of the opportunity. My heart was filled with pride— nothing more. I told myself God didn't care. I questioned why He allowed this to happen to me." Mr. Mayberry pointed to his legs. "I figured I might as well give up. I only thought of myself—not Gracie or Emma. But now I understand. If I had to suffer the injury to be a light to someone else, then it was worth it. Especially if I can share my faith in God."

Blake grinned. "I've never walked in your shoes, but... " As if cold water splashed over his head, he shut his mouth. "I mean… "

"Hey, Blake. Here's the first step I need to take. To not become offended at someone's innocent remark. Please go ahead."

"I was trying to say," Blake's face warmed. "I've never experienced getting shot up in war, but I've struggled with questions, too. Why my grandpa had to leave earth when he did, and now why I miss him so badly every day. I think God alone has the answers, and you've got Him on your side."

Mr. Mayberry's eyes twinkled. "I know I do, and I can't wait to get started. Until you establish our office here, I plan to go to Lakewood. Do you know anything about cars with special accommodations for the handicap? Something else I'd like to do."

Blake slapped him on the back and grinned. "Each time you make progress in improving your situation, you'll have information you can share with another vet."

Mr. Mayberry gripped the wheelchair's handles. "I'm ready."

Blake stood to leave. "I've got an idea about how I'm going to propose. I hope Gracie will be impressed." He shook hands with Mr. Mayberry and headed for his car.

That afternoon, Blake walked out of Oceanview's largest jewelry store into the sunshine which shone as bright as his happy heart. He grasped the bag's handle and pictured the contents in his mind. A beautiful solitaire diamond sat on display within the velvet black box. His second stop at the jewelry store had been as successful as the earlier one when the general manager of MarineWorld Park agreed to his request. Just let him know what day. Blake started his car's motor and dialed the number.

"Hey Blake." The sound of dishes clacking accompanied Gracie's silvery, sweet voice.

"Would you like to check out MarineWorld Park tomorrow. They've started performances again at the whale and dolphin encounters. Besides, we need a day to do something fun."

"I'd love to. In fact, I'll be driving up there every day if I get accepted to the college. I sent in my application for admission and another for a scholarship."

"Great. When do you find out whether you received the funds?" He wanted her to take advantage of every opportunity, yet if she said yes and they were married, he could help her finance her education. But would she be agreeable given Gracie's independent spirit?

"I'm not sure. A few more weeks, I think."

"Okay, I'll pick you up around noon for the afternoon performance." Gracie had no idea she'd see more than trained whales and dolphins.

The sleek movements of the black and white orcas sent goose bumps to Gracie's arms. She tried not to envy the trainers in black wetsuits who enticed the magnificent creatures to sail through hoops, catch balls, and dive and jump at command. Someday she'd be out there performing with the whales—after she finished her program at the college and applied for a job. She peeked at Blake.

He bit his nails and then shifted on the bleacher and glanced toward the exit signs.

Wasn't he enjoying the performance? He'd suggested coming here.

After the show ended, he gripped her hand as they took the steps down the bleachers. "Let's look at the glass enclosure where we can view the divers feeding the fish." He tugged her toward the left exit.

"Sounds good, but the sealion show starts in fifteen minutes. Let's check that out first since the performance is in the next pavilion." She headed toward the exit to the right, gently pulling him along.

Blake lifted his brow, glanced at his watch again, and then coaxed her to a stop in the middle of the aisle.

What was with him? They weren't in a hurry, were they?

He wrapped his arm around her waist and steered her toward the left again.

"But the sea lion exhibit is that way?" She pointed to the right.

"Gracie, I... er, I think we'd like the fish feeding performance better."

Gracie allowed Blake to guide her to the aquarium on the other side of the park. She'd never noticed this side of his personality—the tendency to control her. She wasn't sure she liked that.

At the aquarium, Blake led her down the darkened corridor to the floor-to-ceiling windows. "You'll love this. I promise." He grinned a sheepish smile.

For a moment, she stood, arms folded over her

chest. Then she turned to the glass as a variety of exotic creatures sailed by. No sense in acting like an immature girl. She'd talk to Blake later about how give and take was important in any relationship.

Some of the fish seemed to play chase and others followed the leader. Another with streaks of blue darted around light green, soggy kelp swaying with the water's motion. She closed her eyes and then opened them again. If she didn't know differently, she'd would think she was standing underwater.

Blake rocked from one foot to the other than checked his watch again. He glanced at her, a silly smile on his lips.

She touched his arm. "Do you need to be somewhere? You seem nervous." What was going on with him?

He gave a raucous laugh. "Who me? No, no. I'm enjoying myself."

Which she knew wasn't the entire truth. She'd never seen him this jumpy. Her back to the glass, she turned to stare at his face. Surely those handsome eyes held a clue.

Blake glanced somewhere over her head. Then he reached to grip her arm. "Gracie, look behind you."

She whirled around and drew in a quick breath. On the other side of the glass, a diver glided through the clear water and stopped in front of her. He held a sign in the shape of an orca with words written across the length. *I'm fishing for a proposal. Will you take the bait and marry me? Love, Blake.* She grasped her throat and then laughed.

Blake kneeled on the cement path and held up an open black box with a flawless solitaire diamond inside.

"Will you?"

Her mouth fell open, and she glanced back at the diver.

With the sign propped against him, he placed his hands in a prayer position as if saying please.

The giggles became uncontrollable. "Blake Sloan. I can't believe what I see. You're proposing. I couldn't imagine what you were up to." Prickles raced her spine. "I'd love to marry you."

Blake's smile was as wide as the length of an orca. "You've made me the happiest man I know." Blake rose, slipped the ring on her finger, and kissed her.

From the corner of her eye, she sensed a crowd had gathered. Lights flashed as someone took pictures.

"Excuse me, Blake." The young college man who helped Mom in the kitchen hooked the strap of his camera around his neck. "Would you like photos of the entrance to the aquarium area?"

Gracie giggled again. "Mom gave you the afternoon off?"

The young man ducked his head. "Yeah, but I didn't tell her what I was doing."

Blake shook his hand. "Yes, take as many pictures as you can. I'll get back to you this evening at the inn."

The diver took a few turns around the tank and then gave them a thumbs up.

Blake returned his gesture and steered Gracie down the corridor into the fresh air.

She touched her chest to still her pounding heart. "Your proposal—amazing. How could I say no?"

Blake twisted his fingers into pretzels. "For a minute there, I wasn't sure you'd say yes—but you did. I love you, Gracie Mayberry." He gathered her in his arms again, this time his kiss more passionate than the first. "The sooner the better for me."

"Umm, me too."

"One more thing I want to do before I can get to work on the fishing supply store. I've got to leave tomorrow for a few days. I need to close up my Seattle office." He placed a light kiss on her cheek.

"I'll miss you every minute you're gone." Gracie sighed and tried to shoo away the notion that their plans may not go exactly as they hoped.

Chapter Twenty-One

Monday morning, Blake settled into his chair and glanced around the familiar office. Finishing up a few loose ends wouldn't take long, and he'd return to Cranberry Cove. Maybe tomorrow?

The two floor-to-ceiling glass windows offered a magnificent view of downtown Seattle including the Space Needle. Covering most of the wall behind his massive, mahogany desk, a huge photograph of Dad's fleet of factory ships hung on the wall.

He rested his head in his hands. Memories of his childhood raced back. The times as a teen he spent the weekend with Grandpa and Grandma. Grandpa took him fishing, and Grandma made a homemade cherry pie for when they returned.

He recalled a time earlier when Grandpa worked in this office. He glanced out the window at the gray day, gray like his sentimental heart. A day didn't go by that he didn't miss his grandfather.

He jumped when his office phone rang. Could be a client as Dad always called on his cell. "Sloan and Sloan. How may I help you?" Rain began to pelt the glass windows.

"You Blake Sloan?" A man with a gruff voice barked the words.

Blake sat up straight in the chair. "Speaking. Who's calling?"

"I need thirty thousand dollars in five days." He cleared his throat. "If I don't get the money, somebody down here in Cranberry Cove is going to get hurt." He hacked a brutal cough. "Leave the funds by the west wall of the lighthouse an hour after dark five days from now."

Down here? The person was obviously calling from Cranberry Cove. But how did he know Blake was in Seattle? He hadn't mentioned his departure to anyone except Ryder and Gracie. No way either of them would've passed on information to the person on the phone who threatened him.

"Don't even think about calling the sheriff. And don't try to preach to me about that religious stuff."

Blake's skin prickled. "What are you talking about?"

"Let's just say I got my sources. Listen, I don't have time to gab all day. I'm warning you. Get that money or else."

The line disconnected.

Blake rose from his chair and paced to the window.

The wind beat the glass like the urgent demands from the person on the phone. A chill worked its way down Blake's spine. More than the money, Gracie's safety worried him. And that of the entire Mayberry family.

He dug his nails into his palms. "Lord, what do I do?" Just as Peter almost drowned in the Sea of Galilee but lifted his eyes to Jesus, trusting Him to save him,

Blake knew he had to keep his eyes on the Lord. "In the midst of evil, please work this out for Your good."

Blake walked out of the office and down the hall to Dad's. He turned his head side to side to rid himself of the tension that gathered in his shoulders and paused at his father's office, door ajar. "Dad?" After no answer, he stepped inside.

His father hung up the phone and turned to him. "Blake. How's everything?"

He folded his hands at his waist. "A few minutes ago, I received a call on my office phone. Someone's demanding money, or Gracie's family may get hurt. Someone who knew I was in Cranberry Cove as well as where I work in Seattle. I'll finish getting my office straight, but I need to return later today."

Dad stood and paced toward Blake. "Do you believe your life's in danger? We need to go to the police."

"If need be, I'll go to the authorities there." He shivered, finally admitting the truth aloud to his father. "I'm afraid Gracie's in danger."

"I understand how you care about your fiancé, but please don't do anything to jeopardize your life. Promise me." He gripped Blake's shoulder.

"Don't worry. I've got the Lord on my side."

A knowing grin worked its way onto his father's lips, and he nodded.

Gracie shrubbed the pan with no trace of Shepard's Pie remaining. Her dish with hamburger, mashed potatoes, and corn proved to be her parents' favorite.

She walked out the kitchen door into the backyard. The sun had set though a twilight glow lit the huckleberry bushes bordering the fence.

She closed her eyes a moment and tried to picture Blake. Was he having dinner with his parents in their luxurious dining room, or perhaps he walked the grounds gazing at Puget Sound? She wrapped her arms around her middle, wishing they were Blake's that embraced her.

She needed to go somewhere—take a walk or ride her bike? No. Too late for that. Her phone shifted in her pocket. Call Blake. No, again. She couldn't disturb him as he finished up his business in Seattle.

Ryder. Maybe he'd heard from Blake. For a while, she'd wanted to tell him how grateful she was that he'd prayed with Blake to ask the Savior into his life. She returned to the house and found Mom in the living room. "Can I borrow your car for a while."

Mom thumbed through a gardening magazine and looked up. "Sure, honey."

"Thanks." Gracie's mother hadn't even asked where she was going, for which she was glad.

In Mom's car, she drove toward the wharf and the parking lot. Memories of the handsome guy with eyes the color of coffee and cream made her heart pound. She exited the vehicle and took the steps up to the wharf.

Ryder's usual spot was empty. In the next space, the old, rusted boat bobbed with the waves. No lights shone from the cabin. The scruffy, weather-beaten fisherman appeared to be out.

Gracie paced along the walkway a few times and then turned toward her car. Ryder wouldn't show up tonight. Perhaps he had business in Oceanview or elsewhere.

About fifteen feet from Mom's car, Gracie clicked the locks. She'd go home and read that romantic suspense novel by Fay Lamb she'd meant to start.

She shrieked. Behind her, someone laced an arm under both her shoulders and restrained any movement. Her keys fell from her hands and dropped to the pavement with a clack. Squirming didn't help to free her from the person's clutch.

A man with a deep voice growled behind her. "You better get that boyfriend of yours to bring me the money, or I'll see he'll never go to the bank again." He hissed in her ear. "Kind of hard to make money when you're dead."

Anger overcame any debilitating fear that might've hindered her. How dare this man threaten the life of the one she loved with all her heart. She jerked her shoulders with as much strength as the adrenaline building in her body provided and jammed her elbows into the man's chest.

"Oof." The black shadow of a man stumbled backward a few feet and turned to run in the direction of the ocean on one side of the wharf.

Gracie glanced around and found her keys on the ground a few feet away. Her heart raced, and she attempted to catch her breath. Surprising how weak the guy proved to be. She hadn't seen his face or even the color of his hair.

Finally relaxing in her car, realization struck. As scary as the incident was, she likely had never been in real danger. Whoever attacked her must've been older. Another thought propelled a shiver down her spine. The demand for money sounded like another threat—the ones made by her natural father.

Through the scattering of Douglas fir in the distance, the lights of Cranberry Cove twinkled and danced on the horizon.

Blake tightened his grip on the steering wheel and slowed with the winding road. After ten, and he hesitated to go to the inn this late.

He passed the turnoff for town and headed for the wharf. Ryder might put him up for the night—that is if he was in port. He'd explain everything when he got to his boat.

Thankfully, his friend's vessel occupied his usual spot near the wharf and the museum.

Blake parked and headed toward the trawler.

He tapped on cabin's door. "Ryder, it's me, Blake."

Ryder opened the door and gave him an incredulous stare. "Hey, man. I only got in a half hour ago. I had business in Port Angeles that took longer than I thought. What's up?"

Blake folded his hands. "Can I ask a big favor? I need a place to stay tonight."

Ryder tugged on his ear. "Sure. My couch is available. Come in."

Blake collapsed on the sofa. "It's a long story."

Though he didn't want to, revealing the truth about Gracie's family had become a necessity. "Now that the cops have the stalker, Gracie has another problem. Her natural father is in town, and he's demanding money or, he claims he'll harm her family."

"Oh, man. That's tough." Ryder passed Blake a bottle of water.

Explaining about the phone call this morning twisted his insides into tight coils. "Gracie is pretty sure her natural father is making the threats. I'm not so sure how realistic the man's demands are—or if he'd actually carry them out on his ex-wife, her helpless husband, and his daughter."

Ryder frowned and rubbed his forehead. "I'm here for you, too. I'll do whatever I can until we get to the bottom of this."

"Thanks, buddy." Blake rubbed his tired eyes.

"Try to put this out of your mind for now. God says His mercies are new every morning. We'll try and figure things out then."

Chapter Twenty-Two

"How did you sleep last night?" Ryder picked up his Bible from the kitchen table.

"Great—for the hours I slept." Blake rubbed his eyes. "To tell you the truth, I woke up a couple of times and had trouble getting back to sleep."

"You were thinking about Gracie and her family." He plopped down in a chair across from Blake and rested his elbows on his knees.

"I didn't expect to fall for Gracie when I met her. But her auburn red hair and her spunky personality won me over." Blake threw his hands up in surrender. "I usually don't talk about women like this, but I am now. I love her, man."

Ryder locked his fingers at his waist. "I haven't met the right one yet. Maybe when I'm running a fishing supply store someday." He gave a knowing grin.

"What kind of woman are you looking for?" Blake pinned him with his gaze.

Ryder appeared to focus on the wall behind Blake. "A woman who loves the Lord. One who doesn't lie to me. I had enough of that as a kid."

"Sorry. Sounds like you had some rough times as a child." Ryder's words gave him more of an appreciation for his parents who were always fair and truthful.

"I suppose I'd like to meet a woman who wants a family." Ryder swallowed hard. "I want my son or daughter to experience things I didn't—like a mom whose word they can trust and a father who pays attention to them."

"I'll remind you of what you told me. It will happen in God's timing."

Ryder grinned. "I think about the Word where it tells us to 'Trust in the Lord with all your heart and lean not on your own understanding.'"

Blake squeezed his eyes closed. The message, the same verse from the plaque in his room at the inn... God had directed him to Cranberry Cove.

Ryder rose from the chair, a small Bible in his hand. He motioned toward the front of the boat. "It's a nice day. Why don't we go out on the bow?"

"Sure." Blake stood and followed Ryder.

Outside, Blake settled into a lawn chair adjacent to Ryder's. The seagull's high-pitched screech and the briny, cool air brought a sense of God's creation.

"Listen to this, brother." Ryder lifted his Bible. "'See, I am doing a new thing! Now it springs up, do you not perceive it? I am making a way in the wilderness and streams in the wasteland.' That's from the book of Isaiah."

The words spilled over Blake's spirit. He did feel like God had brought new life into the wasteland of his former existence. "What exactly do you think that means, God is doing something new?"

Ryder took a sip of coffee. "The prophet is referring

to the Messiah God would send to all mankind. But I'd like to believe He's also doing a new work—wait a minute." Something must've caught Ryder's attention. He stood and set the Bible on his chair. "Harry Sallow. He's staring at us and is either very angry or needs to talk."

The same guy Blake offered to help when his truck ran out of gas—the one who'd tried to sell him fool's gold. Blake glanced toward the old guy's boat. "I think you're right. He doesn't look happy."

Harry stood near the railing on his boat, his arms folded over his chest. His downturned mouth looked like a scowl.

Ryder walked to the railing on the port side of his vessel closest to the fisherman's boat. "Hey, Harry. How ya doing?"

Harry snarled. "What's it to you?"

Ryder had been generous with prayer and with money to Sallow. How could he be so ungrateful?

Ryder frowned toward Blake and turned to Harry again. "Nothing to me, Harry. I was just starting polite conversation."

Harry lifted his nose in the air. "You still spouting all that religious talk?"

"Listen man, I only meant to help you."

"You Bible thumpers always want to save everybody. Always trying to take away our fun."

Wait a minute. Blake tensed his shoulders. He'd heard Harry's distinctive gruff voice before, but not as clear as today. Blake snapped his fingers. Harry was the man on the phone who demanded money. Then the second notion struck like a bomb. "Hey, Harry. I need to talk to you." Blake exited the trawler from the stern and sprinted onto the pier.

Harry disappeared around the rear of his boat and out of sight.

Blake picked up his pace. Moments later, a motor rumbled in the parking lot.

Harry sped off in his dilapidated pickup truck and turned out on the main road. The truck's taillights disappeared at the sign pointing to the lighthouse.

Blake rushed for his car. "Ryder, meet me up at the lighthouse!" he shouted over his shoulder.

Gracie glanced at the grocery list on the passenger seat of Mom's car. Carrots, celery, and onions for tomorrow night's stew as well as five pounds of butter and a box of sugar.

Mom had hinted that along with the stew, she planned to make one of Gracie's favorite desserts— pineapple upside down cake. Maybe Mom had ulterior motives, though. Gracie hadn't told her how unhappy she was since Blake had left, but she was sure her mother could read it on her face. Maybe the dessert was an effort to cheer up Gracie.

At Main, Gracie put on her left blinker to turn toward the grocery store but switched the signal off again. Ahead about thirty yards, a Mercedes that looked very much like Blake's pulled out on the road and sped forward.

Blake? She drew nearer behind the Mercedes. The shape of the driver's head, his dark brown hair. The person behind the wheel had to be Blake Sloan. He must've returned, but he hadn't checked into his room at the inn.

The luxury car took a right at the sign to the lighthouse. She remained a few car lengths behind as she wound up the road to the parking lot. One thing she was sure of. At his speed, Blake wasn't going up there for a day of leisure hiking.

After screeching to a halt at the parking lot, Blake hopped out of his car.

Harry's dusty old truck was parked at an angle closer to the woods. The driver's door remained open as if Harry had skidded to a stop and fled.

Blake pushed the truck's door shut and glanced around the parking area. Had Harry continued on up to the lighthouse? At the trailhead, footprints no doubt made today by someone in boots continued along the trail.

Blake sprinted up the path. Why did the old guy go up here? Unless…

Since Blake was sure Harry was the man on the phone, maybe when Harry spotted him on Ryder's boat, he decided Blake had returned to Cranberry Cove to talk to the police—or he figured Blake wanted to make the transfer of funds early. Perhaps Harry thought he didn't need to wait until the end of the week to check the lighthouse for the bribe money.

Or worse, he meant Blake harm and wanted to lure him here.

Whatever the case, Blake had to discover what the

old man was up to. He ran along the trail and through the clearing to the lighthouse beyond. He neared the spot on the other side of the cement structure where the blackmailer wanted him to leave the money. Past the cliff, the ocean waves broke with a crash.

A shot from the cliff zinged close but deflected off the lighthouse. Heart racing, Blake squatted down, not daring to go farther. He was an open target.

He held his breath. Silence. Where was Harry? Blake grunted. He had to get a visual on the shooter. Crouching, Blake tramped closer to the drop-off.

"I missed you on purpose."

An eerie chill crept up Blake's back. He started at the voice coming from somewhere to his front left.

About twenty yards away, Harry emerged from behind a rock near the cliff's edge, a small pistol in his hand. "Can't have you dead—that is if my gun doesn't accidentally slip and shoot you. You couldn't produce the cash if you were." He leveled the weapon toward Blake. "I've changed the deadline. I'll give you until dusk to get the money—or Emma's lame husband will suffer."

Blake firmed his lips and hunkered lower. The cruel words about Gracie's father cut through him like a razor sliced his neck when shaving. Anyone who'd threaten a disabled man was a coward.

His pulse pounded, and his mouth grew dry. He spoke slowly and with a low voice. "What do you have against Gracie? She's a wonderful young woman and a hard worker."

"Listen. I'm not here to chitty chat with you all day." Harry marched closer and swung the gun in Blake's face. "Your little girlfriend's mother didn't bother to ask you for the money, so now I'm going directly to the source. I need those funds, Mr. Money Man. You better go get the cash. And if you try to return with the cops, Gracie's mother will get hurt, too. Even if I have to go to her stupid little house and shoot her. I mean it!"

Blake grumbled as anger swelled within him. This man standing before him had to be Gracie's natural father. "You low life, good for nothing—" He clamped his mouth shut instead of calling Harry the expletives he would've said a year ago. Harry was a sinner in need to a Savior—as Blake once was. "Look, why don't we talk this out. Tell me why you're threatening Gracie and her parents and why you need money."

"None of your business." Harry bellowed. He wiggled the gun in Blake's face again. "This is your last warning." Harry's nostril flared, and he bared his teeth.

Blake lifted his palms in surrender. "Okay, okay." A rustling noise made him glance down at the path in front of Harry.

A large bull snake lay coiled in the dirt, its tail vibrating.

Seconds later, Harry glanced down and screamed. Obviously startled by the harmless snake, he stepped backward, stumbling off the cliff, his gun flying into the air and landing on the beach below.

"Help." Harry grasped a small bush growing on the downward slope, but the roots pulled loose. He dangled, clawing at the earth, and yelled again.

Blake blinked. He couldn't let Harry plunge down the twenty-foot drop-off and likely die when his body slammed onto the rocky shore. "Hold on." Firming his feet on the ground, he reached for the terrified man and grasped one wrist and then the other.

Eyes wide, Harry planted his left foot on the side of the rock-strewn cliff as Blake hoisted him toward the surface. One last tug, and he rolled onto the path at the edge of the drop-off.

"Harry, you scared of harmless bull snakes?" Blake couldn't resist the insult.

"Arrg." He clamped his eyes shut and cursed. "I… I didn't look— I hate snakes." He huffed and lay on the ground breathing hard. Finally, he lifted his squinted eyes to Blake. "You didn't have to save me. You could've let me fall."

"I could've, but then if the situation was reversed, I would have wanted you to save me."

"I don't get it." Harry clasped his head with both hands and moaned.

Chapter Twenty-Three

A shot. Gracie sprinted the last half of the wooded path. At the break in the trees, she took in the scene—the lighthouse, the cliff and then held her next breath.

The old fisherman, his head and chest visible at the cliff's edge, held onto Blake's hands as his body dangled off the side.

With a heave, Blake pulled him over the top.

The man lay on his back panting for air and groaning. What had happened? She couldn't imagine. Maybe the two had taken a walk and the old guy accidentally slid off the side. No, that didn't sound feasible.

Blake bent, his hands braced on his knees, breathing hard. He looked up.

Gracie crept forward to catch a glimpse of Ryder's neighbor, the sixty-something man with a scruffy, graying beard and hardened, downturned mouth.

Her gaze met Blake's, and she continued toward him. "What happened?" She'd never been happier to see him.

"We need to talk." He focused on the man lying on the ground. "Harry is your mother's extortioner. He tried to kill me."

The old guy rolled over and crawled away from the cliff's edge. He slipped, and his head ground into the dirt. Gasping, he lifted up, brushed away the mud that caked his face, and scooted farther away. He fell against the coarse trunk of a nearby oak tree.

Gracie stood over him and stared, not believing what her mind revealed. Realization slammed into her heart as if she'd suffered a heart attack. She gasped, clutched her throat, and then raised her voice. "You are him, aren't you? Robert Brewer."

He rested his chin on his chest, shaking his head from one side to the other and moaned.

As if acid slid down her throat, she gasped. "My father. You're my father."

"Blake!" Ryder raced nearer. "What's going on? What happened to Harry?"

Gracie frowned. "There was a gun shot. He tried to shoot Blake."

Blake shook his head. "He figured he'd try to scare me, but a bull snake came to my rescue."

Ryder's mouth dropped open. "What?"

"Yeah, our pal here is afraid of a harmless bull snake," Blake said. "So afraid, he could've shot the creature but didn't."

Harry yelled and placed his hands on his ears.

Ryder scratched the back of his head. "I've seen them out here before. They do look and act like the rattler. So, what happened?"

"I followed him up here. When I got to the top near the lighthouse, he took a shot at me. He claims he missed on purpose. Not sure if I believe him." Blake jabbed his hands in his pocket.

"But Blake saved him after he fell over the cliff." Pride spread in Gracie's heart. Blake's actions could only be described as heroic.

Ryder stood motionless as if processing the scene. "Unbelievable." He sipped in a breath.

Gracie took a few steps toward Blake and Ryder. "Harry isn't his name. He's my natural father, Robert Brewer." Gracie stared at the man.

"Wait a minute." Ryder shook his head. "Your father? His name isn't Harry Sallow?"

Robert Brewer lifted his head, stared at Gracie, and then muttered. "You have your mother's eyes—and that same fiery red hair, but you have my nose." He paused for a breath. "I knew who you were the first time I saw you when I arrived in town." He shrugged. "I couldn't let on who I was. I had to change my name."

Ryder lifted his eyebrows. "To think, in the book of Genesis, a snake tripped up Adam. Another snake brought about this man's downfall."

Gracie hunched her shoulders. The sight of the older man, sitting in the dirt under the tree, filled her with regret. Despite the way he wronged their family, his demise gave her no joy. If only her father hadn't wasted his life. But what happened hadn't been her fault.

She stood motionless next to Ryder and Blake peering at her father. The rhythmic waves crashing on the beach calmed a bit of the ache inside.

Robert lifted his hardened face to Blake. "You saved me from dying. You're a fool, man. I'm no friend of yours."

Blake slowly closed his eyes and opened them again then grasped Gracie's hand. "Robert called me at the office in Seattle this morning threatening harm to all of us. I prayed that God would bring about something good from the situation. I suppose today the Lord kept Harry from dying and gave him another chance to know Him."

Ryder grinned and slapped Blake on the back. "The Lord used you for His glory."

Robert muttered. "Ryder, I want you to know you wasted your time and money on me." He gave a loud raucous laugh. "I spent the fifty dollars on booze, and I'm not sorry."

Ryder stared at the ground, shaking his head. "Fine, but you can't keep me from praying for you. God didn't prevent you from dying today for no reason. I'm pretty sure He has a plan."

"You crazy?" He scowled at Ryder and then glanced at Gracie. "I know I'm going to jail, but if I could keep on calling your house and hanging up, I would. Had fun scaring Emma's feeble husband."

"Hey! Don't you talk like that about my future father-in-law." Blake shook his finger in Robert's face. "He's a fine man. Twice the man you are. You're nothing but a… " Blake clamped his mouth shut. Then he patted Gracie's hand. "Sorry. I couldn't restrain the words."

"Hmph." Robert sneered and looked away.

Gracie gritted her teeth. "Did you try to attack me last night at the wharf?"

"Sure. I wanted to scare you into getting me the money. You remind me of when I was younger. You got the strength of a bulldozer."

Blake gaped at her. "What?"

Gracie touched his arm. "We do have a lot to talk about."

"Well, this didn't turn out too bad." Harry gave a sardonic laugh. "The casino can't get to me now where I'm going."

Blake lifted his index finger. "Let me ask you something. How did you know where to call me in Seattle?"

"Easy. I heard you telling Ryder you were leaving in a few days. I knew your last name because your buddy here told me."

Ryder cringed. "I'm sorry, Blake."

"It was easy to track you on the web. I didn't have your cell number so I took a chance you'd be at your rich daddy's office. First time I called, you weren't in. I called back."

Blake folded his arms. "I still don't understand. Why did you go to the lighthouse today?"

"I knew you were on to me. I thought I could still scare the money out of you."

Ryder firmed his lips. "Gracie, would you like me to call 911 and notify the police?"

She nodded. "There's no other way. It has to end like this." She shook her head.

Blake slipped his arm around her waist. "It's okay. It's all over."

Robert stood, his slim frame bent, and he limped closer to Gracie.

Blake moved her behind him and folded his arms over his chest. "Don't touch her."

"I don't plan to. I just want to get a closer look at my daughter before I go to jail." Robert's voice wavered.

"I'm not your daughter." Gracie held onto Blake's arm as an anchor. "A daughter is someone who's loved and nurtured by her father. You did none of that."

Robert shrugged. "Life treated me rough. I didn't— "

"I can't listen to this." Gracie shook her head and leaned closer to Blake.

Blake whispered. "He's only spouting off excuses for his own failures."

She nodded and closed her eyes. "In time... "

Ten minutes later, sirens blared from the parking lot and then the rustling of bushes and the sound of footsteps on the trail told Gracie the sherriff had arrived.

Robert glanced at Ryder. "I suppose I wouldn't mind if you came to visit me in jail."

"I can promise you I will." Ryder's downcast face held regret. "I pray that someday you'll realize what a great God that Gracie, Blake and I serve."

Gracie splayed her fingers across her chest as she stared at the surreal scene before her.

With his hands cuffed behind him, her father's head hung low as he trudged along the rocky path. The sheriff gripped his arm and led him in the direction of the parking lot and the patrol car.

"Are you okay?" Blake studied her face.

She fell into his arms, allowing his strong embrace to quiet the horror of the last moments. "He would've died with the fall."

"I couldn't let that happen." Blake moved from the hug and slid his hands around her shoulders. "If I were the one hanging off that cliff, and I had died before asking God to save me, I wouldn't have lived in His presence. I can't judge your father's spiritual status, but if I were to guess, I'd say he wasn't right with the Lord. I'm grateful he has another chance."

Gracie smiled. "From the day I met you… "

Blake pulled her into his embrace again.

Someone cleared his throat. "Excuse me, folks, but I think I'll be going. The sheriff's got this." Ryder twiddled his fingers.

Blake moved a few steps away and rubbed the bridge of his nose with two fingers. "Sorry, brother. I forgot you were still here." Blake shook his hand. "Thank you for backing me up today. I appreciate you. Let me know how I can help you."

"Who knows? One day you may return the favor." Ryder laughed and ambled toward the path and then stopped. "Need a place to stay tonight? I'm in port one more night."

"I might come knocking on your door if I can't stay at the inn."

Ryder waved and disappeared behind the trees at the trailhead.

Gracie led him to the little bench next to the lighthouse. "What's next?"

Blake held her hand. "While I'm awaiting the closing of the space at the wharf, I'll be working on permits for the business. I've asked Ryder to consider running the fishing supply store while I open the DAV facility." He turned his legs so he could face her. "How are you doing? Really? This last month has been hard on you—and your family."

Her heart melted with his concern. "I'm glad it's all over—finally. I never would've believed Robert Brewer under the alias of Harry Sallow was my biological father."

He laughed. "Ryder told me to trust God with my future."

"Your friend is a wise man. I pray he finds a woman he can spend the rest of his life with."

"I have a feeling she's right around the corner," Blake snickered.

Blake's happy mood didn't help to change the concern that came with her thought. She grasped his hand as if it would steady her. What she had to do next might not be easy. "Will you go with me to speak to my parents? I'll call Mom and ask her to let the kitchen assistant prepare tonight's meal. I need to tell them what happened before they see the news that Robert's in jail."

"Yes, of course." He patted her hand. "What you told Robert about being a father was so true. Your real father isn't the man they took away. The man who raised you is the only one who has the right to call you his daughter. He's the one I asked to bless our marriage."

Gracie leaned her head on his shoulder. "Thank you for that."

Blake followed Gracie up the sidewalk to her home. He grasped her arm to restrain her, taking in her wide azure eyes. "Are you sure you're okay?"

Gracie ran her warm hand over his shoulder. "What happened today—Robert getting another chance with God—helped me understand. I need to forgive him because God forgave me. I believe my parents will do the same."

"I know you can, but it will take God's power." He kissed her cheek. "You're a strong woman. When I first arrived in Cranberry Cove, I admired you—mostly for your faith in God."

She took a deep breath, stuck her key in the lock, and opened the front door.

Gracie's parents sat side by side holding hands. Mrs. Mayberry stood. "I knew whatever you had to say was important." She glanced at Blake. "Sit down, both of you."

Blake settled next to Gracie on the loveseat across from her parents. He extended his hand toward her.

Gracie paused, gazing at her parents. She folded her hands in her lap, her diamond sparkling with the ceiling light. "Mom, Dad, you'll be happy to hear the good news though it might be hard. It was for me. Actually, still is." She lowered her voice. "Robert Brewer is in custody."

Mr. Mayberry tipped his head to one side. "What? How can it be. Please, go on."

For the next thirty minutes Gracie explained the events which put Robert in jail. She smoothed her hand over Blake's arm. "Things would be very different if Blake hadn't confronted him."

Blake sat up straight. "I spent last night on Ryder Langston's vessel. Robert was moored beside him, and this morning he came out on his deck and stared at us. Ryder started up a conversation. That's when I recognized his voice from the day before when he phoned me in Seattle to demand money."

Mr. Mayberry moaned. "Oh, no."

"This morning, I followed him to the lighthouse. I knew all of us were in danger."

Mrs. Mayberry reached for Gracie's hand. "I made so many mistakes. One of them was not telling you more about Robert."

"Please, Mom. Don't worry. The weird part was when I saw him up at the lighthouse, somehow I knew the man was him."

"What clued you in?" Blake said.

"I don't know. Maybe the shape of his face. Some sort of instinct."

Mr. Mayberry rolled his chair toward Blake. "You've helped me see my life in another way." He stuck out his hand. "I want to thank you—for everything. For caring about Gracie, for having the courage to stand up for her family."

"I'm glad the mystery's all over." Blake shook Mr. Mayberry's hand. "I can't take the credit. My grandfather always encouraged me to do the right thing and accomplish what God puts on my heart." Blake rubbed the back of his head. "I didn't always listen to the Lord. Recently, my friend Ryder helped me know Him in a more personal way."

"Wouldn't want any son-in-law of mine not to." Mr. Mayberry clapped Blake on the back.

"My grandfather understood why I wanted to start a non-profit to benefit vets and establish my own business—to find my own way in life. I want to serve vets like you." Blake cleared his throat to steady his voice.

Mr. Mayberry threw the blanket off his legs to expose his two stumps and tapped the arms of his wheelchair. "You've given me the courage to do more.

For one thing, to get out of this chair." He glanced at Mrs. Mayberry. "Emma, I'd like to make an appointment with the Lakewood VA office. See about the possibility of prosthetics and some type of employment."

Mrs. Mayberry brushed a tear from her cheek. "Oh, Ted, that's an answer to prayer."

Blake lifted a finger. "If my plans go well, later on you won't have to travel two hours to Lakewood. We'll have a DAV office in Cranberry Cove to service the surrounding communities."

Gracie's warm hand covered his. "You really are willing to leave Seattle for a small town like Cranberry Cove?"

"Yes. The size of the town isn't as important as the people who live here."

Chapter Twenty-Four

Five Months Later

Gracie focused on her gorgeous groom in his light blue tux and tightened her hold on his arm. He smiled as they ascended the stairs to the deck and made their way through the door to the inn's expansive living room. "I love you, Mr. Sloan."

"Not as much as I love you, Mrs. Sloan."

"I have you to thank for the amazing man who walked me down the aisle today." She waved at Dad Mayberry standing at the punch bowl in the dining room. He poured Mom a cup of the sparkling raspberry drink.

The perfect day for a wedding. "I'm glad the weatherman didn't decide to send us rain." Gracie removed her veil and smoothed her dress's satin skirt.

"We could've used the inn's chapel if the weather was bad."

"True. But repeating our vows in the rose garden is something I'll never forget." Gracie sighed.

He planted a kiss on her nose. "Nor will I."

Mom, punch cup in hand, strolled toward her and Blake. "I hope you love the rooms prepared for your reception."

Gracie caught her breath as they drifted into the dining area. White cloths and arrangements of roses with white candles covered the tables. She grasped her throat. "You've turned the inn into a fairyland."

Dad braced himself on his cane and slowly made his way to Mom's side. Taller now than Gracie, he leaned to kiss her cheek.

Her heart skipped a beat as she remembered their trek down the aisle, her arm in Dad's. She wasn't sure who'd supported who, she'd been so lightheaded and excited. "Dad, I'm so proud of your progress using your prosthetics."

"Thanks to this guy and his encouragement." He nudged Blake. "I never dreamed I'd be able to walk again." He shook Blake's hand and laughed. "But I'm still getting used to these walking sticks."

Blake patted his back. "You're doing well. I can't wait for you to start working as a service officer at my DAV office."

Gracie laughed. "You gotta have one first, silly."

He kissed her cheek. "As you know, we're scheduled to open in December."

"And as you know, I'm scheduled for my second semester as soon as we return from our honeymoon." She winked at him.

"Hey, you married people." Ashton, the inn's owner, pushed a baby stroller toward them.

Gracie peeked to glimpse the baby. "Oh, he's so precious. What is he, six months now?"

"Yes, well, five and a half months. James can't seem

to keep his eyes off him." She peered at her baby for a while. "No one will take the place of baby Sammy, but God has been so good in restoring what James lost."

Indeed, God had been gracious after James' tragedy before he met Ashton. "Like God has restored our family."

Mom smiled at Ashton. "I love my new position as general manager of the inn."

"I'm not sure anyone will measure up to your skill in the kitchen, but James and I have our eye on a candidate from Tacoma School of Culinary Arts."

"I'm sure you'll make a good choice."

Ashton replaced the baby's pacifier in his mouth. "We're also thinking about hiring a full-time gardener since James is so busy with his company."

"Here come my parents." Blake whispered in her ear.

With Mr. Sloan following close behind, Mrs. Sloan glided nearer, her high heels clicking on the hardwood floor. She hugged Gracie. "Your wedding was beautiful. We're so happy to have you as a daughter-in-law."

Gracie had no doubt the words were sincere. "Thank you, Mom Sloan. I only wish Grandpa Sloan could've been here."

"I know, dear." She patted Gracie's hand. "We all do."

Blake hugged his mom. "We miss him, but if I had to guess, he's frolicking around heaven with the angels right about now."

"We're very proud of you." Dad slapped Blake's shoulder. "How's your business going?"

"Ryder Langston's my general manager." A year ago, Blake would've had a hard time revealing his personal finances to Dad. Thankfully, that had changed. "I'm making a decent profit. Since he runs the store, I spend most of my time getting my DAV facility established with the state and organizing the office. The DAV branch in Lakewood has offered their help in getting my local agency going. I've received quite a few donations from private individuals and a couple of corporations."

"Good job, son. You know you can invest some of that money and use the interest on expenses."

Blake snickered. Dad had always offered advice, and these days he valued it.

Gracie tapped Blake's arm and grinned. "Tell him about the tourist attraction you're going to bring to Cranberry Cove."

Dad's eyes danced with interest.

"Oh, yeah. I'm beginning seasonal whale watching tours that will leave from the wharf." He put his arm around Gracie. "As soon as my beautiful bride graduates with her associates in another year, she's promised to act as tour guide."

"In between my work at MarineWorld—that is if I get hired on as a trainer."

"You will, honey." Mom hugged her.

Dad cleared his throat. "Well, don't forget your promise to make me and your mom grandparents."

"I haven't forgotten." He chuckled.

Blake slipped his arm around his wife's waist. "I never get tired of listening to the sound of the waves."

"The view is perfect—a fifth floor room facing the ocean." Gracie snuggled into his side.

"We don't have much of a drive in the morning. Oceanview Holiday Resort is conveniently near the airport. You're going to enjoy the view of the ocean tomorrow night even more."

"Hmm. In Hawaii." She tiptoed and kissed his jaw. "Do you know how to surf?"

"Yes." He grinned. "But I think I'll have better things to do." He nuzzled her cheek.

She giggled.

Blake swept her up and headed inside the elegant suite with the king-sized bed. She couldn't weight more than a hundred pounds, he was sure. "I can't wait to start our married life," he murmured.

"I love you, Blake Sloan." His wife leaned her head on the pillow.

Blake snuggled next to her. He'd have her by his side for as many days as God gave them.

The End

Sign up for June's newsletter to get the latest news about her books

June's blog Visit www.Junefoster.com to sign up for her newsletter

Coming next September, book 3 in the Cranberry Cove series. *Christmas at Cranberry Cove.* Ryder Langston retires from commercial fishing and manages Blake Sloan's supply stores. When the owner of the inn in Cranberry Cove hires a new executive chef, Ryder is intrigued by the tall woman with ebony hair who hides a dark family secret.

Juliette Duplay must flee from her French roots and her past when a family member turns against her. She'd like to blend into the American culture but can't escape danger even in the small community of Cranberry Cove.

Can Ryder and Juliette unravel the mystery in time to celebrate *Christmas at Cranberry Cove?*

In case you missed book one: *The Inn at Cranberry Cove* - finalist in Blue Ridge Mountain

Selah writer's contest

Ashton Price arrives in Cranberry Cove, Washington, her pride wounded by her former boss. James Atwood endures punishing guilt after the death of his wife and son. Together, they must discover the mystery that haunts the Inn at Cranberry Cove. https://amzn.to/3sMMLVb

Also, by June Foster The Almond Tree Series

For All Eternity book one

When up and coming interior designer Joella Crawford meets handsome accountant, JD Neilson, he's the man of her dreams—polite and clean cut with strong moral values. He's the perfect Christian man. Or is he? https://amzn.to/3wHEgxi

Echoes from the Past book two

When Dave Reyes, senior pastor of New Life Fellowship discovers he has a six-year-old daughter, his life changes forever. He must reveal the truth to the congregation, but will they fire him and send him away in shame?

Social worker Betty Ann Johnston still grieves over the death of her police officer husband. But when he returns from the grave to torment her, she struggles to maintain her sanity. Witnessing Dave's faith is her only source of strength. Will ghosts from her past destroy her, or will she find hope in the God of the Bible? https://amzn.to/3t4wJXc

What God Knew book three

Tammy Crawford wants nothing to do with her sister Joella's religion but when she falls in love with handsome Dr. Michael Clark, he challenges her long-held resistance. Can two people of different races and beliefs find a life together? https://amzn.to/3fTHIit

Almond Street Mission book four

When Glorilyn Neilson's nineteen-year-old brother, Tannon, goes missing without a trace, she's frantic. Prayer and volunteering at the local homeless shelter in El Camino must fill the time until her sibling returns. But her sapphire eyes and auburn hair inadvertently cause a stir among the male population at the center. Her life changes one evening when she's attacked by a burly vagrant intent on rape in the alley behind the building.

Jeremiah Goodman loves the Lord, but he's homeless. When he witnesses a foul-mouthed vagrant overpowering one of the volunteers at the homeless shelter, he defends her, saving her from unwanted advances.

When Glorilyn offers Jeremiah a way of escape from his impoverished lifestyle, he can't tell her why he must live the life of a vagrant. What powerful secret keeps him on the streets? https://amzn.to/2Q9z8l3

About June Foster

An award-winning author, June Foster is also a retired teacher with a BA in Education and a MA in counseling. She is the mother of two and grandmother of ten. June began writing Christian romance in 2010. She penned her first novel on her Toshiba laptop as she and her husband traveled the US in their RV. Her adventures provide a rich source of information for her novels. She brags about visiting a location before it becomes the setting in her next book.

To date, June has written over twenty contemporary romance and romantic suspense novels and novellas. She loves to compose stories about characters who overcome the circumstances in their lives by the power of God and His Word. June uses her training in counseling and her Christian beliefs in creating characters who find freedom to live godly lives. She's published with Winged Publications. Visit June at June's books to see a complete list of her books.

Find June at:
Amazon Author Page
Twitter
Facebook
June's website

Enjoy these books by June Foster
The Woodlyn Series
Flawless
Out of Control
All Things New

The Almond Tree Series
For All Eternity
Echoes from the Past
What God Knew
Almond Street Mission

Small Town Romance
Letting Go
Prescription for Romance
A Harvest of Blessings
The Long Way Home

The Cranberry Cove Series
The Inn at Cranberry Cove

Christmas Novellas
Christmas at Raccoon Creek
A Christmas Kiss
A Kiss Under the Mistletoe

Devotional
Dancing in a Field of Daisies

Short Stories
Someone to Call His Own
An Accidental Kiss

Stand Alone Titles
Red and the Wolf
Misty Hollow
Lavender Fields Inn
Restoration of the Heart
A Home for Fritz

JUNE FOSTER

Dreams Deferred
An Unexpected Family
Ryan's Father

Made in the USA
Coppell, TX
22 November 2022